So Long the Night

LaJoyce Martin

So Long the Night

by LaJoyce Martin

©1995, Word Aflame Press
Hazelwood, MO 63042-2299

Cover Art by Art Kirchhoff

All Scripture quotations in this book are from the King James Version of the Bible unless otherwise identified.

Printed in United States of America

Printed by

Library of Congress Cataloging-in-Publication Data

Martin, LaJoyce, 1937–
So long the night/ by LaJoyce Martin.
p.   cm.
"A Sequel to: So swift the storm."
ISBN 1-56722-032-0
I. Title.
PS3563.A72486S59   1995
813'.54--dc20

94-48229
CIP

To My Nieces and Nephews

CHAPTER ONE

William's Project

"Caretake that you don't chip that flint into your eyes, Willy." Corine Lewis gave the pan of boiling prickly pears a vigorous stir. Her orb-shaped face was as expressionless as a brown egg.

Resting his chisel and hammer, William looked up at his mother. Sweat beaded like morning dew on his forehead. "I don't care if I *do* put my eye out!" They were brittle, grieving words. "My brother will have a headstone!"

"Jason wouldn't want you outin' your eyesight for him. Nor would I. We've troubles sproutin' faster than goatheads already."

"It galls me when I go to the graveyard and see the fancy markers for the rich folks and Jason without one. My brother was just as important as any of them!" The chisel pinged harshly against the rock, sending another shower of glasslike particles toward the boy's head.

Corine ran the stick she used for stirring around the inside perimeter of the speckled granite pan, then lifted the stick to test the thickness of the syrup by the thin string it made. Lately, she'd cooked any vegetation she could find to keep her family from starvation. Richard, her husband, liked the sticky nectar of the desert pears on his johnnycake. He claimed the cactus berries had the taste of figs, and since Corine had never tasted figs, she couldn't dispute his word. It was food—and that's all that mattered. They had suffered so much privation on this stingy land that it had become a law of life. Anything more was beyond hoping for, striving for.

She spoke again, keeping her voice even as though the words cost her nothing. "I know you're angerin', Willy. But when you're as old as I am, you'll learn that fightin' against death don't bring nobody back." She paused in her stirring to wipe her face with a dingy cup towel. "I've strewed these plains with graves from my own supply. And nary a one had a parson to fling his soul heavenward—nor a mason to hew him a headstone. You learn to bear th' unbearable an' go on livin' an' breathin'.'"

William gave no indication that he had heard her. He worked on with a fierce, tearing energy, putting every ounce of his eleven-year-old strength to the task. The crude letters that took shape from his inept carving were crooked and uneven.

"What year was Jason born in, Maw?" His young-old face looked pale and gaunted. The skinny arms in no way betrayed the wirelike twist of muscles that lay below the surface.

"In 1865. In th' springtide. It was an unforgetsome day. I thought your Paw's hat wouldn't hold th' swellin' of his head—"

The boy ignored the history lesson. "And this is 1889?"

"Yes." She pushed a strand of hair, as dark as bottled

iodine, from her forehead. "Jason saw but twenty-four summers."

Suddenly William dropped the hammer onto the packed dirt floor. Corine saw that his inflamed stare went beyond the open door. It went past the windmill and the ragged outbuildings, past the endless brush flats where the late July heat danced across the sea of sand in shimmering crystal flames. William's gaze seemed to reach into eternity.

Then he closed his eyes tightly and swayed. Corine had the ritual memorized. He had once tried to explain to her that when he did this he was reconstructing a picture of Jason against the darkness of his eyelids. He could see his brother, he said, but Jason was flat and lifeless, like a statue. That's when he'd feel everything crashing down around him, breaking into pieces that he couldn't put back together. Then he would inhale sharply and open his eyes, asking the same haunting question time and again: "*Why*, Maw? Why did it have to happen? Why did it have to be *Jason* who was killed?"

Misgivings raced about in Corine's mind like the mice in her makeshift cupboard. The old sore that alternately festered and scabbed came back to drive a bolt of pain through her heart, yet her black eyes betrayed no trace of the inner turmoil she felt.

It was punishment, of course. Richard didn't like for her to mention the earth gods of her ancestry. He didn't put any stock in them; he believed in the Jesus-God. Yet in the dark of the night she couldn't help but wonder if the wrath of the earth gods played a part in her misfortunes. Otherwise, why had the earth claimed six of her seven children?

It was because of Anna—and those secret feelings of hate Corine had carried in her soul for the girl all these years. She had refused to open her heart to the motherless child, begrudging the unwanted foster daughter food, raiment, and shelter. She had considered Anna the dry rot in the foundation of her own family's happiness.

Eighteen years ago . . . Memories lingered like the grating strain of a note gone sour. Chasing them away was the most threadbare pursuit in the world. They always came back.

Richard and Corine lived in the New Mexico Territory on a section of rented land that belonged to a wealthy rancher named Elliott. They hadn't the money to buy their own land. They were sharecroppers.

Corine couldn't lay a blame of unkindness on the Elliotts; verily, they had gone the extra mile to make the Lewis family comfortable. Though rather less sumptuous than Corine's heart yearned for, life was generous. Reuben Elliott furnished them with a horse and buggy while his good wife offered blankets and clothing for Jason, garments that her two older sons had outgrown.

Then something happened that put a wedge between the two women already separated by culture and living standards. Mrs. Elliott and Corine bore a child the same week. Corine's son died while Naomi Elliott's daughter lived and thrived. Corine became distraught each time she saw Mrs. Elliott's healthy baby. The woman already had three other children—and Corine only one. It wasn't fair!

The envy-begetting circumstance caused Corine to turn inward. She spurned her neighbor's sympathy, insisting that Jason return the woman's gifts of food and supplies. For the next two years, she avoided the smiling landlady and her little Anna dressed in ruffles and lace. The sight of the Elliott baby stirred a festering in her as the bitter loss turned to bile, assuming giant proportions in her mind.

Corine's world shrank to the small area about her cottage. She even switched Jason with a mesquite limb for slipping off to play with the older Elliott boys.

Then came the Indian raid. Cochise, chief of the Chiricahua Apaches, had showed kindness to the white settlers, and they turned on him. That was four years before Jason's birth. Some of the chief's relatives were hung for a crime they didn't commit. After that, vengeance rankled in his blood, and his name became synonymous with terror among the pioneers in New Mexico.

His painted warriors struck the ranch one day about noon. Jason, just short of his eighth birthday, saw them moving toward the Elliott ranch in full war dress. The Elliotts were working in their fields, unaware of the danger.

Thinking fast, Jason ran into the Lewis cabin and grabbed an old muslin sheet. He had heard somewhere that the Apaches were skittish and superstitious. He draped the sheet over his body like a ghost and ran toward them flapping his arms and making moaning sounds.

They had already killed Mr. and Mrs. Elliott and the two older children before they saw Jason and fled in fright. The third child, a girl, disappeared and was never seen again. Jason found baby Anna in the house, just waking from her nap. He gathered her in his arms and took her to his mother.

At first, Corine was delighted. But her motives for

wanting the child were far from noble. She thought there would be financial rewards. *They* would be rich now. The big square-shouldered house would be theirs—with its pegged pine floor, the high-backed tapestried chair, the chest of drawers, the double bed . . . and the oil lamp with the tasseled shade that she had long coveted. When she learned that the deed to the Elliott property had been lost, her interest in rearing the "stray child" (as she called Anna) waned.

Corine wanted nothing more to do with Anna. The child's fair skin and cotton-hued hair contrasted sharply with her own thick black braids. The resentment that Corine had harbored against the porcelain-white Naomi Elliott, her neighbor and landlord, went to seed. Her hostility spread to all light-skinned children. Anna must go.

However, by now both Richard and Jason had bonded to the little girl. "I found her," Jason argued, "so now she belongs to me." Richard vowed that she filled an emptiness left by the departed child of their own.

"A child is a gift of God," Richard said, "to be loved and provided for, whether my own or another's."

When Richard and Jason gave Anna special attention, a jealous torment came to set up camp in Corine's heart. An intangible wall came between them and her, leaving her on the other side feeling cold.

She immediately began to plague and ply Richard to leave the territory and move to the populated east, reasoning in her mind that Anna would be left behind. "I would feel safer in another part of th' country," she whittled. "Who is to say th' Apaches won't strike again?"

Richard insisted that he wished to stay and manage the Elliott ranch until some legal disposition was made of it. "A relative of the family will show up eventually," he said.

Corine became obdurate. The land would never be theirs. "We need somethin' we can pass on to Jason," she said. "We must have land of our own. It will give us back our losses." She nagged Richard until he could bear it no longer.

When they started east, Richard announced that they would take Anna along with them. Corine said no, they should leave her behind with a local family in case some of her relatives did show up.

"We're takin' her, I say, Corine." Richard's word prevailed. He could be as stubborn as a mule if he set his mind on something. "Unless Anna goes, none of us go."

They broke down on the bald plains of Texas, and there is where they had been ever since. They had seen drought-stricken summers and skimpy winters; the land was dry and tight-fisted. They'd eaten rabbit, antelope, and wild birds . . . and now prickly pears.

The prairie, with its mad blizzards of flying dust, racing tumbleweeds and cacti, had now become home—and the burying ground for four premature boys in the past fifteen years. Of the children born on this wild stretch of nothingness, only William had survived to blot up Corine's affection.

Anna grew up to be gentle and soft-spoken, an antonym for her foster mother's clumsy manners and bitter tongue. As the months turned to years, Anna grew taller, fuller, and more beautiful, making Corine more conscious of her own homeliness. Both Jason and Richard tried to protect Anna from Corine's ire, hoping to shield the girl from the knowledge that she was unwanted by Corine.

Corine steadfastly insisted that Anna not be informed that she was not a bonafide member of the Lewis family. It wasn't to spare Anna's feelings; she didn't want Anna to know that Jason wasn't her brother lest the girl get romantic notions as she grew older. She kept Jason from any private conversation with the girl.

Then quite unexpectedly, a solution had presented itself. A wagon of travelers going from California to the Oklahoma land run sought shelter in the Lewis's stucco hut during a blinding sandstorm. Among them was a young widower left with a baby. According to his mother, Esther Horn, he sorely needed a wife to replace the one he had lost. "My son needs someone to nurture his ailing and orphaned infant," she said, "and someone to bind up his grieving heart."

Anna! Corine seized the opportunity to pawn the girl off to the sojourners, soothing her conscience with Esther's promise of a plushy life for Anna in the new land of paradise to which they were headed. Anna could even stake claim on land herself! The relief that flooded Corine was like the satisfaction of a craving appetite.

Anna didn't want to go. She objected that she did not wish to marry Lesley Horn. She implored Corine to allow her to stay. But in spite of her pleading, Corine had helped her into the wagon with a shove too hard for friendliness. She wanted to be rid of Anna before the girl discovered her family history.

With the monster of jealousy caged at last, Corine had been content while awaiting the impending birth of another child. Now she had Jason and William and her husband . . . and Richard must never know that Anna had left unwillingly.

Then Jason went into Lubbock and never returned. There had been a shootout at the tavern, and a young man was killed. When nobody came to identify the body, the county buried him. Richard went into town the following week in search of his son and came back with the dreadful news that Jason was dead.

Corine's life, so selfishly arranged, had been devastated. *It is because I sent Anna away.* A burden of guilt leeched onto Corine's mind. It corroded, hollowed out, ate away. *The ill I had in my heart for Anna caused all this trouble. The gods are making me pay my debt.* A swelling pain in her chest blocked the escape of her tears.

She bore a tiny girl that night, so fragile that she was sure the infant would draw few breaths, if any. She couldn't separate the pain in her heart from the pain in her body. But the child struggled and lived, and Richard named her Jana for Jason and Anna. That had been six months ago. . . .

The tribulations had not stopped. Since then, their best cow had died, taking with her the hopes of future calves. Everything, it seemed, was coming apart. Would the debt never be paid? *If I knew where to write*, Corine told herself, *I'd send Anna a message of apology. Then mayhap the plague would be stayed.*

"Why did Jason have to die, Maw?" repeated William vehemently. "He was so *good*—the best brother a boy could have! When he told me about honesty and truth, he made me *want* to be a better person—" A cry choked in his throat.

His outburst awoke the baby. She stretched her tiny hands toward him. Like a pulled puppet, he ran to her, scooping her into his bronzed arms. He seemed to forget the clawing question. With this bundle of sunshine, the harshness of life was debarred, only its warmth and tenderness admitted.

"Oh, Jana!" he cried. "I just wish Jason could have seen you! He would have loved you. See the headstone I'm making our brother? I want to have it done before winter, but I can only work on it when you are asleep because I wouldn't want any of the flying gravel to get into *your* pretty little eyes!"

She blew slobbery bubbles.

"And the next time I'm in town with Paw, I'll get some empty spools from the lady at the millinery and make you a toy! Willy will make a wonderful dolly for Jana. It will be a dilly of a dolly." He muzzled her neck and made her laugh. "Dilly-dolly. You'll have a *dilly-dolly!*" He danced about with her.

"Dee-daa," she cooed.

"Did you hear her, Maw? She said it! She's talking! She said it as plain as you please. She's not only the *sweetest* baby in the world, she's the smartest, too!"

"Nobody can bring Willy out of th' doldrums but Jana," Corine told Richard that night. "Lawsy! I never seen a kid so crazy about a baby sister!"

CHAPTER TWO

Escape

It took a few days for Anna to realize that she had actually escaped from Lesley Horn.

One moment she was sitting in the Oklahoma Station Hotel in her wedding dress, her heart drowned in hopelessness, awaiting the arrival of the soul-scarred man she despised. Her head throbbed with the pressure of racing blood. Waves of cold fear crashed onto the shores of her weary mind. Lesley had gone for the parson. As she watched the door with dread, a merciless vise began a slow twisting inside, tightening her with a terrible anguish until she felt one final twist would be too much.

The next moment, Jason had appeared to rescue her from an unwanted marriage. She thought she must be hallucinating. Surely her mind was playing a cruel trick on her! Yet in her heart there was a small fire of hope.

He had hurried her out the door, and they had fled, fearful that Lesley would follow them. The jilted groom would be angry and his rage, Anna knew, provided an alarming sense of energy. His supply of venom was inexhaustible.

"I've spent many days searching for you," Jason had said. He had been eager to tell her of her family history and that he loved her, not as a sister but as a sweetheart. But she already knew that she was not a member of the Lewis family. She had found a diary that belonged to Lesley Horn's deceased wife. The journal brought to light some other startling facts. Lesley's wife was Anna's own sister—the one who had disappeared in the Indian raid. Lesley's baby was Anna's niece.

Her sister's memoirs recounted the Indian raid. Jason's name was there. The deed to the New Mexico property was in the trunk with the diary. Anna was anxious to share all this with Jason.

Lesley Horn did follow them. He found them in Purcell that very evening. He had been drinking. Anna tried to forget the moment of terror when he pointed the gun toward Jason and then her, but it was tattooed in her memory.

"This is your wedding night," he leered, his face so close to hers it was a visual collision. She could smell the alcohol on his breath. "Come along with me to the parson—and bring the brat." He gestured toward the baby. "We've got Jason Lewis, the pauper, here now and we'll do it up right! Ha! Ha!" She remembered the taste of fear in her mouth, the shivering weakness in every part of her. If Jason were killed, it would be her fault.

Her hopes struck a partnership with sunset and went down. Convinced that all was lost, Anna's first thought was that she would rather die than marry Lesley Horn. Let him pull the trigger! Let him end the misery of her ruptured dream! A thousand thronging sensations came and went while her mind darted from one dead end road to another.

She gritted her teeth to stop their nervous chattering, pushing back a rush of nausea. She gave Jason a look of silent apology, a look that gathered up all the love within her and bore it to him. Neither spoke, yet each told the other a thousand things.

Her mind went to Deana, her sister's baby. Whatever the cost, whatever the personal sacrifice of her own happiness, she must live to care for her niece. It was the least she could do for a departed sister whom she could not even remember. She could not abandon the child to the whims of such an evil-hearted man, a man who considered the precious child nothing but a burden. She must stand between Deana and Lesley's certain abuse.

"Let's get a move on to that preacher man!" thundered Lesley. "Cooperate and you'll have nothing to fear. Trot or you're shot."

The confusion accelerated when a tawdry woman stepped from the shadows and with a soggy kiss claimed Lesley's attention. Her black taffeta sleeves hissed when she moved her arms. "This is my *wife!*" he lurched, presenting the buxom gal. Did he expect Anna to be his *second* wife, the victim of a bigamous marriage? Such a thought had the quality of a nightmare.

"Miss Holy-Holy, I'm going to *make* you marry the penniless pauper, Jason Lewis, this very night!" He gave a raucous laugh. "And as part of the grand hoax, you will take the brat and see what it is like to honeymoon with a kid on your hip. In fact, you can dance your way into eternity with her hanging to your skirts. Marrying that church mouse is your punishment for running out on me!"

In a staggering march, Lesley led them, military fashion, to the storefront church and demanded the preacher to "tie the knot good and hard" so there would be no slips. He didn't want Anna coming back for his land, money or good looks, he sneered. She had forfeited all her fortune when she ran away. It would be sweet revenge to see her go back to the "poorhouse" and the sandstorms from where she had come. "And I'll even pay the preacher," he grinned, throwing out a roll of ill-gotten bills.

When the drama had played itself out to such a swift and delightful conclusion, Anna felt she had been holding her breath for the entire hour. She recalled the surpressed mirth that broke into rapturous peals of laughter when she and Jason were out of hearing distance of the church, now legally man and wife.

"Happy punishment!" Jason straightened his face and tried to look solemn. Then they were in each other's arms with Deana snuggled between them, trying to contain their heart-bursting thanks.

"He made a mistake," Anna said. "We're *not* paupers. We have love—and anyone who has love is never bankrupt."

"And we have land," Jason reminded, "if we can just get there."

"The Elliott land. What was it like, Jason?"

"In a little boy's mind, everything seems vast and glorious, Anna: a quiet corner of wonder and enchantment. It's a world by itself. The house—if it's still there—seemed a mansion to a seven-year-old. But whatever it is or whatever it isn't, we have each other, and that's what matters."

"Yes . . . oh, yes, Jason!" She nestled closer, basking in the sweet scent of her impossible happiness.

It took them four days to work their way south across

the Red River to a town called Byers Bend. In the years to come, she would remember the trip's blurred swiftness in terms of scant meals and never enough sleep. The weather was warm and they camped in places abandoned by the land rush pilgrims, foraging for nuts, berries, and roots they could use for food.

They met with late stragglers who had been beset with problems and missed their chance for free land in the Oklahoma Territory. "You're *leaving* the promised land?" they were asked by the northbound travelers.

"Yes," Jason answered. "It holds nothing for us. My wife has property in the territory of New Mexico, a country where the sun spends the winter. We're working our way that direction."

With the Red River between them and their tormentor, Anna felt better. Her mind unclogged as though a broom had swept it clean of the devilish man who probed his pitchfork into the sorest of spots.

But they were indeed penniless, as Lesley had reminded them.

CHAPTER THREE

Delay

"We can't go on without food, Anna."

"What will we do?"

"I'll look for a job."

"Where will we—live?"

"I don't know."

At Byers Bend, Jason applied for work on a bridge construction project. Mr. Butler, the foreman, hired him on the spot. "You look work-brittle," he said. And when Jason asked about lodging, Mr. Butler opened his home to them.

Anna tried to hide the apprehension that started in her throat and ran down to form a cold lump in her stomach. What would it be like to take a baby into the house of a stranger? Some people—like Lesley and his family—considered children a nuisance. Then, too, Jason would be gone for long daylight-to-dark hours and she would be alone with a woman she didn't even know.

"Anna." Jason looked into her troubled eyes. Even their silences seemed shared and understood. "We won't be here long. As soon as we've enough money for the trip,

we'll move on. Try to endure, my sweetheart. I'll make life
better for you as soon as I can. If I had known we would
get married so *abruptly* . . ." His boyish grin kindled a
small, tight smile of her own. His arm came gently around
her shoulder, offering comfort and cheer.

She should be grateful for Mr. Butler's generosity in
offering them a bed, Anna reminded herself. He didn't
have to. It would be better than camping under the stars,
their bodies providing food for mosquitoes. Her mind
flapped about like a washing on a line.

Surrounded by the invisible wall of Jason's quiet
strength, she braced herself for the new unknown. The
other world—the sunlit one where love was easy—would
have to wait. *When we get to our land, everything will
be wonderful.* To reassure herself, she repeated the
thought over and over with more inflection of challenge
each time. In New Mexico, she would have a home of her
own. . . .

In answer to Jason's knock, Mary Butler padded to
the door, her cheeks flushed and her hair dampened by
exertion. She was in her late fifties, broadly and harmo-
niously built. Her face showed few signs of her age. From
behind her, the smell of freshly baked bread joined the
scent of wood smoke and ironing. Anna took refuge in
Jason's shadow.

"Oh, you must the be the *Lewises!*" Little gutters
around her mouth turned to a smile, her manner a mask
of polite inquiry. "But Theodore didn't *tell* me. A *baby!* I
understood that you were *newlyweds!*"

The only safe ground that Anna knew was silence.
With mental fists she beat down the rising anxiety within
her. The world seemed to make no room for the young,

the helpless. Apparently it had always been thus. She'd read in the Bible that the infant Jesus was relegated to a stable. Had nothing changed in the hundreds of years since?

"Her name is Deana," Jason said, offering no explanation for the child. Deana turned somber eyes upon Mary Butler. Then her rosebud mouth broke into lovely bloom, lassoing the woman.

"Oh, it's just *too* wonderful!" crooned Mrs. Butler, who emphasized a word in every sentence. "A real *baby!* And she *likes* me. Oh, you darling . . . Oh, but I will become *attached* to her. I'll surely weep when she leaves.

"Oh, but *do* come in out of the heat and make yourselves right at home! You'll never find a *warmer* welcome anywhere." She ushered them into a room of hand-braided rugs and pine furniture. Anna thought she would never again see anything so grand. "And your *precious* mother, little Deana. Why, you do look plumb drained and tuckered, Mrs. Lewis." The solicitude was real. "I'll watch the baby while you sleep and *sleep.*"

Hedged about with Mrs. Butler's kindness, Anna succumbed to the dragging weariness that came over her, reminding her that she had slept little since her escape from Lesley Horn. "Thank you, Mrs. Butler. You are *too* kind, I'm sure." She didn't notice that she had stolen Mrs. Butler's habit of accenting words.

"Please call me Mary. And I *hope* you can bear my smothery mothering. You *do* look so young, and since Theodore and I were never blessed with children who could bring us grandchildren, Theodore says I try to mother everybody in the *county.*" She talked so fast that her words bumped into one another.

25

"Anna could stand a little mothering—and Deana a little grandmothering," Jason nodded. "We've been on the road for many hours—"

"Oh, I'm so *glad.* Oh . . . not that you're weary, but that God would allow *me* to help."

The Butler home was cool and comfortable. Mary fretted that Anna needed "some meat on them bones." "Gotta keep body *and* soul on speaking terms," she said, clucking over her charge like a mother hen. Was their feather mattress soft enough? Did they need a larger water pitcher in their room? Were the pillows the right size? "Theodore'll be glad to fix up a wash basket on rockers for a *cradle.*"

Mary's household spun in a cyclone of activity. A monstrous slice of her day was spent in cooking. She started the morning with a gargantuan breakfast that would "put an *all-day* lining in a workingman's innerds." Many of the dishes she cooked, Anna had never tasted.

She set a new batch of sourdough bread every other day. "That's the most wondrous bread I've ever tasted," Anna complimented.

" 'Tain't hard," Mary said. "Just boil a couple of taters, strain them and put the *juice* in a wooden keg along with a cup of sugar and enough flour to make it pasty. Then set the keg over hot water and put the lid down *tight.* It's ready to make into bread in twenty-four to forty-eight hours. That is, if it doesn't *rain.* In damp weather, it takes longer."

Mary never stopped moving. "Nature doesn't *like* a vacuum and neither do I," she told Anna. "Idleness is the devil's greenhouse where he plants all *sorts* of bad seeds." When she wasn't cooking, Mary made smocked dresses and tiny doeskin shoes for Deana. Anna watched and learned.

"Deana will be the best-dressed child in the New Mexico territory," Anna laughed. "And no place to go!"

"There'll be places to go, dear," Mary said. "People are moving *west* by the droves. You mark my word, it won't be long before some of the very ones who made a run for Oklahoma will turn around and run *back* again. There'll be something to lure them! Then there'll be shops and socials and *churches* to dress up for."

"I hope so. I've never been to church—" She hesitated, not wanting Mary to think her a heathen.

"Your Maw didn't take you to church?"

"My mother was . . . killed when I was only two years old. We—that is, I lived with Jason's family on the caprock of Texas, and we were so far from *anywhere*. I'd never seen a town until last year when I traveled to Oklahoma with—with—" Painful memories stopped her. If she hadn't coughed suddenly, a sob would have forced itself into her throat.

"Oh, you poor, *poor* dear." Mary eased back into her chair. "Then you have never had the chance to be *saved*?"

"Saved? Oh, yes! Jason saved me from—"

"I mean your *soul*."

"My soul?"

"Yes. Saved from sin."

"I—I guess not. Sometimes I pray—"

"Oh, that's a *start*. A good start. You seem so *sweet*. But sweet isn't good enough to get you into the kingdom. And *good* isn't good enough. There's a man in the Bible who kept all the commandments, but Jesus said he *still* had a lacking. You must be in the *kingdom*."

"The kingdom?"

"God's kingdom."

"I'm afraid I'm very ignorant—"

"Oh, *lamb!* You are not ignorant, you've just never *heard.* God sent you to me. We don't have a church here at Byers Bend yet, so I hold prayer services once a week for the neighborhood ladies right here in my parlor. We tote a tune and study God's Word. You are welcome to attend and learn about God's plan for your *eternal* redemption."

"I . . . I think I'd like to come."

"Oh, but you *must* come, dear. That's part of God's plan for landing you here with me."

On Friday morning they arrived, young women and old. They were a mixed, odd lot. Some brought hymn-books; all brought their Bibles. Anna had no idea what to expect. A tiny chill pricked the skin along her arms. *I should have made some excuse not to attend,* she thought, *but now it's half past too late.* She sat in a corner, hoping to lessen the chances of being noticed. But as the meeting progressed, she found her mind struggling relentlessly to grasp every word. That night she told Jason about the strange meeting. "They sang and prayed and told about how God had saved them," she said. "Some of them swooned. Jason, are you saved?"

"Saved?"

"Do you have Jesus in your heart?"

"I don't know if He's in my heart, but He's my friend. I . . . I think I'm saved. But sometimes I feel like there's something missing—something that I can't quite put my finger on."

"I feel that way too, Jason. What do we do?"

"We keep searching until we find the answer—just like I kept searching for you until I found you."

"Mary said that seeking the truth and finding it is the only satisfaction in life that nothing can take away."

"I agree with her, Anna. When we get to our home, you can stitch that wisdom on a sampler for us."

The next day while Deana napped, Anna looked up the list of Scriptures that Mary had given her. The process was slow and some of the words failed to convey any meaning to her. However, one particular verse spoke directly to her heart: *"Blessed are they which do hunger and thirst after righteousness: for they shall be filled."*

"Dear God," she prayed, "I know so little about You, but I want to know more. I want to be saved. I am hungry and thirsty for Your righteousness, Your Spirit inside of me—"

A warm wave rolled over her, and when she came to herself an hour later, she supposed that she had been in a trance. The words she was saying were unintelligible. She felt clean and whole and happy. She could hardly wait to share the amazing experience with Jason. The words of an old philosopher she had met in the grub of humanity on the banks of the Red River came back to her: *A joy shared is doubled. A sorrow shared is cut in half.*

God. Jason. Deana. She'd found a rare completeness.

CHAPTER FOUR

Decisions

The job lasted two months and paid well. Theodore Butler spurned any money that Jason tried to pay for room and board. "You've paid well in the joy you've brought to our home," he said. Both he and Mary had grown attached to the baby, and Mr. Butler urged Jason to stay on.

"There'll be another project open up soon," he promised. "God never lets me rest for long. I guess He knows I'd get lazy!" He grinned and inclined his head toward his bustling wife. "I wouldn't want to get slothful like Mary here."

"You take care of your chickens and I'll take care of mine, Theodore," Mary responded in a good-natured banter.

Theodore sat whittling out a butter paddle. "I was thinking you could stay on through the winter, Jason, and pull out next spring with enough money to put a house on that land you're pining for."

Jason, never one to sit and fold his hands waiting for a bird in the bush that might take wing, responded.

"Thank you, but we have enough money to get to our land, and that should be sufficient. We're hoping that the house is still there; it was a sturdy structure sixteen years ago. Deana will soon be a year old—and although we could ask for no greater kindness than you have shown us, my wife needs a place of her own. Every woman should have her own flower patch."

"What better time for a flower garden than next spring?" Theodore was unwilling to give up.

"I'm hoping that we can get settled before the weather turns. I'd like to have the land readied for the spring planting."

"You must use your own scales in life to weigh the things that really count," conceded Theodore. "No one else can weigh them for you."

That evening, Anna and Jason went for a walk in the nearby woods to discuss their departure, leaving Deana to Mary's care. They found a fallen log screened by brush and sat quietly together.

"Do you want to stay the winter here, Anna?" Jason asked.

Slivers of sun filtered down through the trees that cast lacy shadows on the ground. It was hot. It seemed the parched earth gave back at day's end all the blazing heat it had siphoned during the earlier hours.

After an uneasy pause, Jason spoke again. "If you want to stay, we will."

Anna's mind twisted and turned like a trapped animal. In leaving Mary, she would be leaving the only real mother she had ever known. At Mary's house there was security and safety—and the prayer services that she had learned to depend upon. Was she strong enough in her new-found faith to walk alone? She had grown so much, come so far! A silence fell over her and lasted longer than a silence should.

"If you had rather wait until we have more money—"

"No . . . no, it isn't that, Jason." She tried on a little laugh that didn't fit. "It's just that it's hard to . . . to leave the *known* for the *unknown*. Mary has been a great example to me. Everything is done with such efficiency here. I . . . I want to have you and Deana to myself. I want to be a good wife and mother. But I'm afraid that I'll never be able to do things like Mary . . ." Everything she had ever felt welled up in her, choking her—fear, love, hope—all for Jason and because of Jason.

"Anna! Anna!" His smile was full of understanding. "Mary fills her life with busyness to staunch the ache of childlessness. You will not be like Mary; I neither want nor expect you to be. No two women do things alike. She has her way and you will have yours. I have no qualms about whether you will make a good wife and mother. You will please me, and that's all that matters, isn't it?"

She buckled on a smile as a suit of armor to ward off more tears. "I'm glad God sent us here. I've grown so much and learned about so many things. Mary has been a marvelous teacher but I . . . I think I'm ready to get on with our own lives, Jason. I can't always lean on someone else."

"That's my girl!"

"Will we go by and see your maw and pa before we settle?"

"Yes, I would like to go by and bid them farewell. When we get to our land, we'll be busy, and it may be years before we see them again. It won't be much out of the way to go by. And that would only be fair to William," he added.

"Your maw won't be happy about our marriage, will she?" The deep breath that Anna drew held a shudder somewhere underneath.

"No, but I'll tell her that I had no choice in the matter. It was Lesley Horn's doings. Marriage or death." A sparkle just short of a glitter flashed in his brunet eyes.

"She might set out to . . . to prove it isn't legal or something."

"Maw knows nothing about the law. And you were never adopted into our family. The fear that Maw will separate us is emotional baggage that you can leave behind."

"I don't want to come between you and your family, Jason."

"Precious Anna, you *are* my family now. I will forsake father and mother for you." He held her in the terrible realization of her fear to be guarded, loved, and battled for. "I only hope Maw isn't . . . rude to you."

"Why didn't she like me, Jason? I tried to be a model child. I never gave her a sass."

"Maw couldn't forgive your mother for having a healthy child when her own baby died. Jealousy can warp a person until that person can't see truth from lies, vengeance from loyalty. You were fair and beautiful . . . and you posed a threat."

"A threat?"

"Maw knew that I loved you from the day I found you when you were two years old. If a child can fall in love at eight years old, I did. I think Maw feared losing my affection to you."

"But . . . but I can love both of you, you can love both

of us, and we can all love each other."

"Of course we can. But Maw can't understand that. She doesn't comprehend the magnitude of love. I'm not sure she is acquainted with love at all. She resented you while you were growing up, and she will resent you even more now since . . . since you've taken me away from her."

"Didn't she realize that you would wish to get married sometime?"

"She wouldn't let herself think of my leaving. You see, so many of Maw's children bypassed the world that she tried to cling to the ones who did survive."

"I think I understand, Jason. She's been through a lot. The mind makes its own defenses. I . . . I hope that she isn't worried about you."

"Maw wouldn't be Maw without a fret. However, I left word with Joshua at the blacksmith shop to tell them I had gone to the Oklahoma Territory to check on you."

"What made you decide to come to my rescue, Jason?"

"I was so concerned when I didn't get a letter in the mail after all that time. I knew if all was well, you would write as you had promised."

"I did write."

"I didn't get it."

"Lesley Horn said that he would mail the letter for me at—" A dawning crept over her face. "Oh . . . he never mailed it."

"Naturally he wouldn't have. I was his rival."

"I'm glad you didn't get it. If you had, you wouldn't have made the trip."

A slow dusk was closing as they turned back toward

the house. "Now about the trip, Anna—I plan to send you and Deana ahead on the train. It will save many hard miles for you and the baby."

A worried frown tightened Anna's heat-flushed face. "No matter how long it takes to get there, Jason, I don't want to be separated from you." Her mind clawed wildly at an enemy she could not see. "I'm . . . I'm scared. Why can't we all go on the train together?"

"There is no need to be frightened, love. Trains are marvelous conveyances and great time savers. I must return Paw's horse to him."

"Couldn't we put the horse on the train with us?"

"Ole Jesse wouldn't like that. He'd buck and snort and kill himself or somebody else."

The choking fear still swirled and galloped around Anna's heart. "Deana is a good little traveler, Jason. . . ."

"It is a great distance to Lubbock, Anna. More than three hundred miles. Remember how long it took us to get here from the Oklahoma Territory? *Four days.* And that was a short distance. I can travel much faster, and with more ease of mind, alone."

"How long, Jason?"

"I'll hurry."

"Oh, Jason!" A hidden spring of tears, an intruder lurking behind her eyes, tried to break through.

"Now don't cry, darling, or my heart will drown in your tears. It's but twenty miles to Wichita Falls. I'll put you on the train there and you will go as far as Lubbock and wait for me. We will go to Maw and Paw's together."

"Where . . . where will I stay in Lubbock?"

"Remember the hotel where Paw and I lodged when we had business in town that required more than one day?

You'll have the money to stay there until I arrive."

"How will I know how to get there?"

"Ask at the depot and they'll tell you. You can hire a carriage to drive you to the hotel."

"Is the hotel . . . safe for the baby?"

"It is a decent place. The discomfort will outweigh the danger, I'm sure. There's a small dining room. And you won't have to walk far to get anything you might need. I'd be worried about you if you stayed anywhere else."

"Is . . . is it like the place we stayed the night Lesley Horn found us?" A tremor slid down her spine.

"It is much more modern. The first night Paw and I stayed there back in the 70s, I thought we were rich. I still remember the down-soft pillows and the framed picture of the grand hotel itself looking down on me from above the bed. A thick, padded rug stretched almost to the walls. And it has two clean bathrooms. I remember lying awake wondering if heaven could be more lavish!"

"But I'll be . . . *alone* in a big city!"

"This is where we must trust God to protect you, my sweetheart. I know that you will be very careful. Lubbock is growing, and with its growth comes crime. The day I left, a young man was shot in a tavern—"

Anna wrinkled her nose. "I won't be in such a place. I promise."

"I wouldn't have been there either except that the postman was inside and I needed to ask him about the mail." He grinned. "You drove me there!"

"I'm glad it wasn't *you* who caught the bullet."

"God was watching over me. It went against my grain to go into such a low place and He knew it. The shot went right past me and downed a young man about my age. My, but I don't see how anyone could *enjoy* such a den of iniquity! We've only one life to live, and it seems anyone would want to live it clean and honest. Why would one want to cheat or gamble or lie? Like I always told William, there are only two choices in life. Either you're a real man or you're a false one. There is no in-between. A real man takes the high road.

"Some men have no truth in them. A man without truth is not a free man. He is bound by his own self-deception. The truth is what makes a man free."

"True, Jason. And now that I've found my real man, I don't want to leave you. What if—?"

"No what-ifs." He lifted her chin and looked into her clear sapphire eyes. "Remember our Scripture: *What time I am afraid, I will trust in thee*. You must trust the Spirit we've just made acquaintance with to guide me and keep me safe. Unless I miss my guess, He has a long full life planned for us together!"

He bent to kiss her, and it happened again. While his lips lingered on hers, the earth swam in a dizzy spin.

CHAPTER FIVE

Adjustments

When Anna reached Lubbock, she felt limp and exhausted. Her body still seemed to be moving on the clacking train. Her mind was an attic, jumbled with things that kept falling about her. She tried to recall Jason's last tender kiss, his last hurried goodbye as the conductor rushed her on, but found that she couldn't remember any clear sequence of events. Every thought dissolved into shapelessness.

A drizzle of rain fell, fine and warm, driven by a thin, spastic wind. The moisture added to the ovenlike heat. Deana's damp hair curled in tight ringlets along her forehead.

Anna stood under the eaves of the depot with a bleak hollow in the pit of her stomach, her senses shut against the panic that tried to engulf her. In the crook of her right arm, she held Deana, and in her left hand was the portmanteau Mary had given her for the trip. It held the dresses Mary had made for them, the Lewis family Bible, her sister's diary, and the deed to the New Mexico property. Her money lay in her deep skirt pocket.

She looked around, bewildered, trying to recall Jason's instructions. She must make sure her aloneness didn't advertise itself.

"Carriage, ma'am?" A weather-burned driver made a slight bow at the waist.

"Uh, yes, please."

"Your destination?"

"The hotel."

"Downtown?"

"Y-yes, I guess so. Is there another?"

"There are others, but a lady would choose the town hotel. The one *below* the tracks is full of lice and mice and boozers." With an imperious air, he appraised her, his eyes shrewd and bargaining, making her recoil inside.

"Oh. Yes, of course, thank you. The downtown hotel is the one with a tearoom and two clean bathrooms, is it not?"

"None other." He helped her into the conveyance, his eyes remaining tightly on her.

The air was light here on the high plains and its prickling sensation brought back a phantasmagoria of memories: prairie dog holes, deceptive mirages and storms—savage sandstorms with their blazing, parching terror. The mental flashback started a strange throbbing in her throat. *Oh, Jason, if only you were here to calm the racing of my heart. . . .*

The buggy lumbered down Main Street and stopped before a tall building crowded with windows and constructed of hewed stone. Its imposing bulk used up a whole corner of the block. Wagons were scattered along the side of the street with horses shifting in their harnesses. The city, loud and busy, seemed to be running a dozen ways at once.

With such a crowd, it seemed that the whole world was in town that day. Anna sorted the human sea before her into layers. There were the painted women and raffish men on the bottom. Then there was a common, but still respectable class of cowboys and ranchers and farmers' wives. The big people were at the top: bankers, merchants, teachers—those with silk top hats, ivory-headed walking sticks and golden watch fobs. She didn't seem to fit in any layer.

The carriage stopped with a shudder, and the driver helped her down and into the busy lobby of the establishment. He stood waiting.

"Thank you," she mumbled, ill at ease with his closeness and hoping that he would move on. Still he stood rooted at her side.

An unfocused feeling of confusion threatened to suffocate her. Why didn't the man leave? He expected something, wanted something. What? The answer was vague, lost in the pandemonium.

He cleared his throat with an artificial cough. "Ah . . . we do charge for our services, Madam. If you don't have the cash . . . ah . . . we could make other arrangements for payment perhaps?"

"Oh, I'm . . . I'm sorry, sir." With an agony of misgiving that brought a deep blush to her face, Anna reached into her pocket and gave him twice his usual fare. *Oh, Jason, I don't know how to conduct business in a city!* There was no one to help her, guide her, advise her—and had she divined the men's jaded inference, she would have wept for the world's decay.

The driver bowed again and favored her with a sly

41

smile that twitched his wisp of a mustache. "The name is Lucius. Any time I may be of service to you while you are in the city, madam, please let me know. And in *any* way."

Anna turned quickly away from him. His eyes had the same hungry look that she had seen in Lesley Horn's eyes, the same untamed violence. They brought back memories she wanted to leave unstirred. When she glanced back, he had edged away, vanishing into the throng.

She paid her room rent for a week and put her name on the smudged hotel register beside the other scrawled signatures. She wrote "Anna Elliott Lewis" as neatly as she could and then, at the last minute, thought to add "Mrs." to the front of it.

"*Mrs.* Lewis, is it?" asked the man at the desk. He had a weak chin and a pale puffy face, but the set of his shoulders suggested he felt he took up a great portion of room in the universe.

"Yes," Anna said. "My husband will be joining me in a few days." Then a jagged pattern of fear zigzagged across her brain. She had revealed too much! Jason had warned her to be careful. Cities were not safe places for a lone woman who talked too freely. "That is, he will be here . . . any time, actually."

But the hostelier didn't appear interested in any explanation. He stashed the money away in his cash drawer and gave her a long skeleton key. "Second floor. Third room to the right. The bath is at the end of the hall. Guests are allotted one towel a week."

It was a lovely room that overlooked the city street—and nicer than anything Anna had ever seen. This would be her refuge; tomorrow would be an easier day. *Jason, you are taking such good care of me even though you are not here!*

The high poster bed wore a spread of purple satin that reminded Anna of dark, wet grapes. In one corner was a roll-top writing desk complete with an inkwell and a quill. Paper and sealing wax were provided for letters to be posted. A straight-backed chair, a spider rocker and a dressing table finished out the furnishings. And yes, there was the picture of the grand hotel mounted above the bed just as Jason had described it. She could almost hear his voice now, and she was swept with a longing for him. She felt near him; then the awareness faded. But it had comforted her.

Deana had fallen asleep on Anna's shoulder. Anna, well spent herself, lay the child down and fell across the bed like a dropped boulder. Her last conscious thought was that perhaps if she slept, the long hours ahead without Jason would shift and form a pattern that would make time less tedious.

Then peace came with a gauzy veil blocking out the future. It was a blissful, dreamless sleep, and she awoke to Deana's whimper. Where was she? Why was she here? Where was Jason?

Sight and sound swam back, pushing her onto the shores of reality. *Oh, yes . . . Lubbock. The hotel.* The baby must be hungry!

How long she had napped she did not know. The dusty light, distilled by the chintz curtains, gave her no clue as to the hour of day it might be. She sorely needed a time-piece.

"I am in Lubbock waiting for Jason," she reminded herself aloud. "And I haven't unpacked a thing!" She felt rather foolish talking to no one in particular, but the spoken reminder gave her something tangible; holding onto it kept her steady.

When she opened the suitcase to hang her dresses on the clothes hook, she discovered that Mary had slipped a tin of soda crackers and a bag of dried fruit into the luggage. That was just like Mary! A pang of loneliness for the motherly woman came with such intensity that Anna tasted the bitter salt of tears before she knew she was crying. And she would probably never see Mary again!

The trip had taken a heavy toll on Anna's emotions. She hoped that Deana would be satisfied with the fruit and crackers and that she wouldn't have to venture out of the room until morning. She didn't wish to see anyone. She wanted to think, to examine the fragile moments she had shared with Jason without breaking them. She wanted to count back through the sunsets and sunrises they had shared. She longed to look inside the Bible and find their verse again: *What time I am afraid, I will trust . . .* It was in the Psalms and she had it marked.

She'd have some mental adjustments to make. She had Jason to wait for, and Deana to care for. Both of them needed her to be brave. She would face her problems courageously.

From somewhere came a calmness. Tomorrow, she decided, she would buy some thread and crochet doilies for their new home using the stitches that Mary had taught her. She would embroider scarves and cup towels and pillow shams. And she'd make Deana a little goblin's cap for the winter. She wouldn't give in to anxiety or discouragement. She would pay love's price and no longer ask why. Nothing that was worth having came easy. One must face and make the best of uncontrollable happenings.

Her days would be filled with purpose and thrilling plans for the future!

CHAPTER SIX

Weather

"You'll want to follow the Red River as far west as possible, then drop down to the south," Theodore Butler told Jason. "In this kind of heat, it is important to stay near water. One can get in trouble quickly crossing country when the small streams have dried up. It has been a powerfully dry summer. . . ."

Theodore and Mary had insisted on going with Jason to see Anna off. Jason felt his whole being heavy with the weight of his disappointment. He had wanted a private farewell—a lingering kiss—when he put Anna on the train. They'd had such little time to themselves! Now Jason must return to Byers Bend with the Butlers and wait until morning to start out himself. He was impatient to be on his way, but he had been trained to respect his elders, so he acquiesced to the Butlers' wishes. He hoped that his horse would be able to carry all the food that Mary had already packed for his trip. He had rather travel lighter, but how could he refuse Mary's generosity without offending her?

"The sky is a funny color this evening," mentioned

Mary on their way home. "A sort of seashell gray. And the air is as restless as an irritable sleeper! I believe weather's a-coming."

"Mayhap it's the herald of autumn," Theodore said. "Everybody's rushing the fences for a break from this heat. Especially me."

The day drained into a long night and Jason slept shallowly. The room seemed as airless as a tomb. Each time he aroused, he whispered courage to himself, waiting for the sun. He could hardly bear the bed empty of Anna.

Morning came, but the sun didn't. A deep gray haze masked the daylight, and Jason heard a low, distant growl like a dog under the porch. Then a vein of lightning splintered the sky. He raised the pull shade and watched the rain streak in with a tearing violence in driving sheets almost parallel to the ground. His eyes traced the great flat drops running down the drizzle-streaked pane.

The emptiness in Jason's stomach wasn't all hunger. His mind, trained to deal with realities, fought against the abused hopes of beginning his journey at dawn. Theodore said that he would need to stay close to water. He'd have no problem now.

Two suns are missing today, Jason thought. *The other is Anna.* She lit up his whole world. What his life was worth without her could hardly be measured by the cheapest coin. They'd shared a few brief and perfect days. As the years passed, life would change as they grew older and wiser. But still the glow would linger. Still the light of their love, in the blackest night, would warm him.

He heard Mary bustling about, preparing breakfast. The banging of pans on the iron stove melded with the clashes of thunder. Between the noisy outbursts, he could hear her humming a hymn. He joined her in the stone-floored kitchen with its black beams crisscrossing the ceiling.

"Theodore was *wishing* it would cool," Mary said. "It cooled, all right. Problem is, the half-grown cool spell doesn't know what to do with its *energy*. This part of the country is a miracle in sunshine, but a *disaster* in the rain. It's because we're so close to the rivers, Theodore says.

"There's a limb off the elm tree and leaves scattered *everywhere*. My flowers are bent over and dragging in puddles. Of course, they'll straighten, come a little sunshine. They're bounce-backers.

"Have you looked out? Rivers are running through the yard in *all* directions. The mud's a-gleaming and the rain's still falling solid and hard. Hasn't done this all summer. We may be in for a *spell*."

Jason opened the back door. Water ran from the edges of the roof in isinglass sheets. "Looks like I won't be traveling this morning." The struggle showed in the muscles of his face.

"I'd say not," Mary commented. "But you've a son's welcome *here* for the duration, you know."

"How long do storms usually last in this part of the country?"

"One can never predict," Mary answered. "Mayhap just a few hours or mayhap a seven-day dread. I always allowed that the true gift of God is the courage to *endure*. He gives us strength to deal with even the *worst*."

"If I lose a day, I lose that of which my world is made,"

49

Jason grinned. "A day with Anna, I mean."

"Oh, the hurry-up of youth!" chuckled Mary. "My Mammy always said when trouble arises one must think of a *bird* caught in a net. The more it struggles against its problems, the more it gets enmeshed. If it is still and looks for a hole, keeping its strength and wits about it, it has a better *chance* to escape." Spilled water scalded up in tiny frying sounds from the stove.

"I . . . I'll try to find that . . . that hole in the net."

However, as the hours dragged on like a tortoise, the wall of rain hanging from the black-bellied clouds strained Jason's nerves near the breaking point. He felt as if a cord were being drawn tight around his chest. Would the deluge never stop? Would tomorrow never come? If the true gift of God was courage to endure, he sorely needed that gift now.

He could have been happy, he reasoned, but for Anna's absence. He had sent her on ahead one day too soon. The irony of it was too cruel to bear. Together they could have endured, yea, even enjoyed, the coziness of the weather, the fellowship of these friends. But he had sent her away to Lubbock against her wishes, and now he must cope with his own impatience, with his boredom . . . and with his longing for her.

Just when the storm appeared to be clearing, new clouds formed. By nightfall, it was bad again. Jason made up his mind to start out the following day, rain or shine. The going might be slow and wet, but he would be moving toward *her*. He waited for dawn to chase away another night so that he no longer had to try to sleep. He missed Anna's nearness with a dreadful ache.

An urgent knock and call at the front door brought

Jason to his feet, grabbing for his clothes. Had something happened to Anna? Every sensation heightened. Theodore was just ahead of him, blundering into wakefulness.

A wild-eyed woman stood there with a blanket drawn about her shoulders, shaking all over. "Mr. Butler, please come quickly! The river is drunk on floodwater and the new bridge you just built is gone. The swell will reach our house any minute—and my children—oh!"

Theodore waited to hear no more. "We must run, Jason!" He plunged into the darkness with Jason at his heels. An inner strength as solid as a second skeleton filled Jason with purpose. He no longer felt like a chip floating aimlessly with the current. God—and this nameless woman—needed him. Each minute was precious.

The men deposited four shivering children on high ground before the house floated away on the crest of a wave. "Oh, thank you!" The mother's tautness snapped, and her breath came back in a gushing rush, leaving her empty.

"Thank God that I had Jason to help," Theodore said. "Without him, we would never have gotten them out in time."

Jason and Theodore worked all day, evacuating families and finding lodging for them while the rain struck spitefully at their faces and widened the river into a flood plain. Under the whip of time, they did their best to save furniture, livestock and food. When they toed off their mud-clogged boots that night, relief outweighed weariness. They had saved several lives.

"Jason," Theodore said, "I can't tell you how glad I am that you were here."

"I am glad, too, Mr. Butler."

"I hate very much to ask, but could you stay and help me rebuild the bridge that washed out? Several families are cut off from civilization without it. You are the best worker I've ever hired—" He combed his hair with his fingers. "If you don't feel that you can stay . . . well, I just don't know what I'll do. . . ."

Jason jerked his head so quickly that a bone made a cracking sound in his neck. "I'd be glad to stay, but Anna wouldn't know—"

"We'll send her a telegram. And we'll wire her some more money for her keep there—"

"I sent most of the money I had saved with her. She'll have . . . enough. But of course we must notify her at once."

"We'll get a message out tomorrow. You wouldn't be able to cross the Canadian River in that direction anyhow. The sandbar crossings will be whirlpooling between banks. During a rainy season like this, the floods scoop out hollows in the banks and the current carries with it the debris jolted from the bottom. It would be too dangerous to attempt to ford that turbulent and unruly giant for some time yet."

There was no hiding anything in Jason's face. Worry and disappointment chased each other around. His mouth opened and closed like a clam, checking the spate of words fighting for release. An indefinite period of time away from Anna? Like a war-torn area, his heart was in shambles. He gave a bare nod.

"You're saying that you'll stay and help me?"

With absolute certainty, Jason knew that there was but one thing for him to do. "I . . . you've been so kind to me. When I needed help, you gave it freely. I can't leave you in a lurch . . ."

"I'll make it well worth your time, Jason. I will pay you double."

"No, I wouldn't expect extra pay."

"But it's the least I can do to compensate for my unfairness in keeping you from your lovely wife and baby."

Jason stayed, and Anna dominated his thoughts—thoughts that helped him bear the days more easily. He would dream of her at night, then awaken to the reality of the present. She would be fine, of course. She'd probably accept the inevitable better than himself. He had provided her with quite enough for a long-term stay at the hotel.

Each day dawned with its own distresses for Jason, but the trial that weighed the most was his separation from his beloved Anna. He marked the days off his mental calendar, each day bringing him closer to her. Surely it wouldn't be long. . . .

They worked for tortuous, back-breaking hours on the bridge. Mary kept their clothes laundered and mended, their meals prepared. Her only complaint was that she missed Deana, the "grandbaby" that had been hers so fleetingly.

"It's a shame Mary didn't have a dozen children," Theodore told Jason. "But mayhap God figured her love would drown them!"

Then one evening they found Mary trailing clouds of glory through her imagination. "One of the prayer service ladies brought a government notice," she said, setting the platter of fried potatoes in front of them. Some secret activated the smile lines embedded around her mouth.

"And guess *what*, Theodore—"

"My guesser is too tired to work, Mary," her husband rejoined. "It never was any good, really."

"No, it wasn't," she agreed. "In fact, I used to *worry* about your guesser, but then I figured God gave me to you so you'd not have to guess. Well, the Children's Aid Society is looking for *homes* for children from New York in rural America. These are immigrants and orphans and crowded city children. They're called 'streeters.' The poor babies *live* on the streets and sleep in doorways and cartons. Some of them get their food by stealing or selling their little bodies. . . ." She blew her nose and took a few deep breaths.

"And what can we do for them, Mary? I'd be glad to help."

"We could take one or two or *three* of them, Theodore. We live in rural America, don't we?"

"You mean bring them here? To our home? Why, Mary, we're old enough to be grandparents now."

"There's no stipulation on *age*, just a 'reasonably good health' requirement and a place for them to sleep. They'll send them by rail if we pay the fare. Oh, Theodore! They've been doing this since *1854* and we've just found out about it! We could have had a house *full* of laughing children all this time!"

"It would be a lot of work for you, Mary."

"I'm not a delicate peach blossom to be blighted by the first frost, Theodore. I'm a strong tree with branches for *many* birds."

"Then send off for some of them, Mary. And if it works out well, we'll put in for more."

Mary's face changed from disbelief to doubt to ecstasy.

"You mean that?"

"Why not? Stingy we'd be to have all this plenty and let little children go begging."

"My Theodore! You've not only the world's biggest *feet*, you've the world's biggest *heart*, too!" she crooned, and suddenly Theodore became as shy as a schoolboy looking at his shoes.

Mary's face glowed with the light of a woman walking into her own dream—a dream buried so long ago that its substance had turned to dust.

Here is a special woman, thought Jason. *A woman with deep reserves of kindliness in spite of having used a great deal. . . .*

This opened his sentiments to Anna, always the first and last page of his mental volume—the special one in *his* life with a sweetness beyond words, beyond everything. . . .

They'd grow old together like Theodore and Mary. There would be children and grandchildren. The thought filled Jason with a wild, spreading joy.

CHAPTER SEVEN

The Telegram

Anna slid in and out of sleep, feeling that a thousand ages of time were wedged between her and her beloved Jason. Had it only been four days since she'd left Mary's house?

The world was still dark except for the pale oblong of early light where the window was. Sounds of birds announced the start of another morning. The temperature was rising, like bread in an oven, but summer was at its height; it would turn cool soon.

The street below was almost deserted. Out the opening, she could see the hanging lanterns, pinioned from metal wall brackets, shining down on trade signs swung over each shop door. A delivery boy hurried down the boardwalk with a piece of paper in his hand. She tried to imagine what it would be like to be looking out the window and see Jason rushing toward the hotel. The thought brought a joyful torment. How could she wait another moment, another day to see him?

She hoped that they might spend a night or two here before going on to see Richard and Corine Lewis. How hard it would be for her to call Corine Maw, now that she knew the difference! What a relief it was to be delivered from Corine's wordless persecution, her silent coldness. Whatever abuse she might be called upon to endure during their short visit in the Lewis home would be bearable because of its impermanence.

Dawn ripened, and Anna slipped out of her cambric nightgown—a part of the new wardrobe Mary had made for her—and into a gingham dress. Deana would awaken soon, and they would go to the tearoom for breakfast. The meals weren't like Mary's, but they met the challenge of simple survival and the prices were fair. Deana liked the cornmeal and molasses pudding, and Anna was at home with the cook's simple fare.

Anna's ears picked up a noise in the hall. As it came nearer, she distinguished it as footsteps. Someone must be moving into one of the adjoining second-floor rooms. She and Deana had had the floor to themselves since they'd been here, and she was thankful for that. She wouldn't mind neighbors now—if they were the right kind.

There was a tap on her door. She remained very quiet, groping for the caution Jason taught her. The rap came again, a bit firmer. "Mrs. Lewis?" Her mind seemed to go numb; she felt unprotected.

"Mrs. Lewis, if you are there, I have a telegram for you."

A flicker of fear nudged her like the first twinge of a toothache. No one knew where she was except Jason. Why would he send her a telegram? Telegrams were expensive and seldom sent for sentiment. Had something happened to Jason?

She opened the door and took the yellow sheet from the boy she'd seen rushing down the street. Tension strained her slender frame. The messenger's face told her nothing.

"Thank you." The words went limp in her mouth, but she added quickly, "Do . . . do I owe you anything for bringing it?"

"Nothing, ma'am." He bowed. "The telegraph company takes care of my salary."

She closed the door and read the words in a gobble, one eye on the first word and the other reaching to the last. She reread it until she knew it by heart, forward and backward. It spoke of love. HAVE BEEN DELAYED STOP OCCUPY UNTIL I COME STOP LONGING FOR YOU STOP JASON. Reading it brought a swelling hotness behind her eyes, a lump in her throat.

Deana awoke, wearing her wide-eyed morning look. "Deana! We heard from Daddy!" Anna held the page up for the child to see.

"Da-Da," Deana mimicked, clapping her small hands together.

Anna felt segmented into slices, a part of her exhilarant with happiness because of the message and another part protesting against the delay in seeing Jason. Then there was the part of her that recognized the need to reappraise and reconstruct her life so that the added time would be less tedious. He had given no indication as to how long the interruption of his plans might take or what had delayed him. *Wireless messages are such bone-bare things*, she thought.

She dressed Deana, and they had their breakfast in the hotel's eatery. As they started back through the lobby, a boy with a face too young to know a razor waved a newspaper toward her. "Read about Miss Lilly Langtry . . . a scent of scandal . . . the world's favorite perfume," he hawked. "Oranges for health, California for wealth! Read about Doctor Mayo's wonderful hospital. . . ."

Anna found herself fascinated by the boy's sales pitch. Who was Lilly Langtry? And what about the wonderful hospital? A sudden desire to purchase a paper seized her.

"Can you read, ma'am?" The boy stopped his chanting.

She colored. "Y-yes." Richard had taught her to read well.

The salesman started to move on, continuing his rhetoric: "Oil in New Mexico going for a dollar a barrel. . . ."

The words "oil" and "New Mexico" hummed in Anna's ears. "How much?" she called after him.

"A dollar a barrel," he repeated in his recorded cylinder voice.

"No, I mean how much for a newspaper?"

"One for a nickel, two for a dime. Better be quick, I haven't much time. . . ."

"I'll take one, please." She groped in her pocket, her fingers counting out the pennies.

"Will you want one tomorrow, too?"

"Yes, every day, please."

"Same time, same station. All the news in the nation. . . ."

Reading would help to use up the hours until Jason came, hours that weighed heavy on Anna's hands. The telegram said, "Occupy until I come." Jason wouldn't want her to sit idly. She would enrich her mind so that she would be a better conversationalist for her husband. No one wanted a dull, stagnant wife. *Like Corine Lewis.* The thought came unbidden and with it a sense of shame that it had come.

While Deana took her midmorning nap, Anna absorbed every word of the newspaper. She had never owned one, and since she'd bought it, the messages seemed hers personally. Lilly Langtry, whomever she was, commanded a front-page story. She had been diagnosed with measles a few hours before her opening play "As You Like It." The opening was postponed. Now she had caught influenza and was seriously ill. Was she dying? Had her hair fallen out? Would she be crippled for life? What would her fans do if she could not return to the stage?

Anna failed to comprehend the world's obsession with this one woman. For shame! The attention given her bordered on worship! The nation was making a goddess of her, a mere earthling!

Anna's eyes moved from news item to news item. She was intrigued with the information. She could sit in her room and travel all around the world. And all for five cents.

Only a small column on the back page shed any light on the discovery of oil in the New Mexico Territory. Keystone Oil was leasing land, and the price of the black gold had shot to a dollar a barrel. Anna was disappointed to learn no more.

At the foot of the page were the ads. Someone wanted to sell a setting hen as soon as her eggs hatched out. Another wanted to buy a "nigh new" wagon. There was an address to send off for a free seed catalogue.

When Anna had read the newsprint from front to

back, her eyes were weary from strain, but Jason would be proud of her. She was "occupying," waiting for him . . . for the click of the door . . . for his quick familiar footsteps. . . .

She dropped the newspaper and pulled the telegram to her breast. It was her tangible link to her husband.

CHAPTER EIGHT

The Bite of Poverty

The August heat burned itself into Richard Lewis's dried-to-jerky cheeks. He splashed the wire-handled bucket into the windmill's wooden trough, letting his thoughts take him to all the days they had saved and scrimped so they might have something in the dim future. He'd squandered his few years of health and vigor on this flat and featureless desert where there was never enough food, never enough water—and never enough hope. Now gray sand filled the hourglass of his face. He was crumbling from the inside out.

Looking back, Richard supposed that the bottom dropped from his pockets the minute he settled here. He had forgotten what it was like to live a single day without want.

Poverty bit deeper every week. Richard gave a long, slow sigh. *I guess I should have gone to the Oklahoma Territory with Philip Horn last year when he invited me*, he thought. *Then mayhap I'd still have Jason and I'd be close to Anna. If only I could budge Corine!* He doubted they could survive another winter here with no resources. The quicksand of financial ruin was swallowing him, and he was angry at his own ineffectiveness against it. All his ambitions were pressed into a tight little package of the past.

William's voice reached him from a distance. Quickly, he reached down to reclaim the forgotten bucket, finding relief in the dailiness of life. William must not catch him racked by his private anguish. The quality in a child that made him blind to obstacles should be nurtured as long as possible. Richard sensed that this virtue was tarnishing in William already.

"Can I help you, Paw?"

"I was just dipping up some water for the night, Willy. Thanks anyhow."

Layers of clouds held the sunset's hues of spilled watercolors. Once Richard would have thought them beautiful. Now his judgment was marred by the effort of resisting the waves of hopelessness.

"When are you going to town next, Paw?"

Richard's answer held a deep tiredness. "I don't know, Willy. There are things we sore need, but—"

"But what, Paw?"

"We . . . I'd have to buy on credit, and I can't bring myself to do that."

"How much would it take?"

"Three dollars would get us enough ground corn, lard, and beans for a month, but think what that would amount to for a *year*. Thirty-six dollars! Borrowing is easy. It's the paying back that's hard. If we go in debt this month, we'll be twice behind the next. At the end of every rash action is a consequence."

"But we gotta feed Maw and Jana, Paw."

Richard felt crushed between the hammer behind him and the anvil ahead. "That's true, Willy. I've spent many sleepless nights trying to work out a plan for us. And now . . ." he turned his head and looked out over the non-speaking wilderness with its grave cloth of sparse weeds, symbols of a thousand dreams turned brittle. He winced, finding the telling too painful.

"Jason said a real man was brave—"

"Ah, yes, Willy. Real men are brave. But there's never been a man alive who hasn't faced fear. Bravery is to keep on going against all odds even when you're terribly afraid. A grown-up man feels fear just like he did when he was a little boy, only he reacts differently. Fear isn't the same as cowardice. A coward will turn tail and run when the going gets tough."

"Then fear isn't wrong?"

"There's no sin in fear. If there was, my soul would be branded and doomed."

"I've been worried about Maw. And a little bit afraid, too."

"So have I."

"Her flesh is wearing away, isn't it?"

"I'm afraid so. I thought it was because she was nursing the baby, but she has weaned Jana now and she is still wasting. I don't like the rusty rasp of a cough she has, as if her throat was scoured with barbed wire. She needs a good tonic."

"She's been failing since Anna left and Jason died. Her clothes are getting too big for her and she just picks at her food."

"Yes. Your mother is not one to show grief on the outside. That's the nature of her people. But her heart has been so pierced that ordinary feelings no longer register."

"I feel so helpless, Paw."

"It would help if Corine could believe more in our God. We must be gentle with her, Willy, and try to lead her. . . ."

"How can we convince her that God is real?"

"She said once that if she could see something that God did just for her, she'd believe. We'll pray that He will . . . do something. And in the meantime, we'll do all we can to lighten her load."

"I've been taking care of Jana for her."

"Thank you, son."

"And oh, Paw, Jana is such an angel baby! I don't know what I'd ever do without her! I love her so!" He spoke as if all his heart were gathered into that single bundle of words.

"You've been doing a good job all the way around. I'm proud of you . . . and Jason would be proud of you, too. I . . . I wish he was here to help us make some decisions about the future. He could always come up with a few good, strong nails of logic. Lately, my thoughts are nothing but a tangle that gets me nowhere."

"I wish he was here, too."

"One thing is certain. We can't sit here and let your mother die a slow death. If I only knew what to do!"

"What choices do we have?"

"I could sell this place for what little cash it would bring, and we could pull up stakes and go somewhere else. That is, if Corine would hear to it . . ."

"Would anybody buy it?"

"Oh, yes. The big ranchers out of Lubbock are waiting like vultures to snap up any little plot from down-and-outers like me—as if they were buying a bag of flour! Then they sell for a sinful profit. But what the buyer doesn't know is that he's buying a dream in place of reality."

"What was it like, Paw, before you came here?"

A brief light, not quite defeated, leaped into Richard's eyes. "We lived in a heavenly place—a fertile valley held in the palm of God's own hand. Anything would grow there: fruit, vegetables, grains. Your Maw even had flowers. We never went begging for food, and the winters always smiled."

"Then why did you come to this sandstorm place?"

"It was your Maw's idea to make a move. Being man of the house, I should have stood my ground and refused to leave. But I would never have had a minute's peace, and I'm a peace-loving man. Quarrels are terrible things; they don't sleep. They stay awake to add and subtract with a gnawing desire to be in the right. Then the trouble starts to multiply.

"I didn't want to quarrel with my wife. Corine had a fearsome torment after the Indian raid and couldn't have a quiet night's sleep. What I couldn't make her understand is that people cannot escape by running away, because most difficulties arise from inside and no one can leave himself behind.

"I left there because of . . . her. Here's where our wagon broke down, and I was able to work out the mortgage on this place with my bare hands. We never got up the money to go on."

"Couldn't we go back, Paw? Back to the smiling land?"

"The land didn't belong to us—"

"But it would be Anna's now, wouldn't it? She wouldn't care if we moved back! She'd probably be glad!"

"That's rational thinking, Willy. You remind me of Jason with your smarts. I'm sure Anna *wouldn't* mind. She'll be married to Lesley Horn now and will finish out her days in the Oklahoma Territory with plenty."

"And mayhap Maw has forgotten her scare after all these years."

"Chief Geronimo surrendered in '86, and Billy the Kid was captured back in 1881. I don't think there would be any danger for Corine. She might not want to leave these graves here, though."

"She has a grave back there, too, doesn't she?"

"She does. A wee boy lies beneath the sod. I hadn't thought on that. She might be homesick for that first grave. We could talk to her. If she knew that *you* wanted to go . . ."

Richard saw William's lower lip tremble. "I'll hate worse than the plagues of Egypt to leave Jason's grave behind, but the living are more important than the dead." His expression mirrored mixed emotions. "I was thinking if you could take the headstone to the cemetery for me in the wagon, I'd have done my duty by my brother and I'd be free to go. I got it finished today."

"I'll be honored to do that, Willy. It was noble of you, my boy."

"You know, Paw, when some men die, it don't make much of a bulge in the graveyard. But when a man like our Jason goes, it leaves a shadow across the ground too long to think about."

"Yes, men like Jason put their notch higher on the tree than the others."

"When can we go to Lubbock?"

"We can go next week."

"I need to stop by Mrs. Wright's millinery shop, too. I want to pick up something there."

"You don't have any money, Willy. And I won't allow you to go crediting."

"It won't take money. I want to get some empty spools to make Jana a dilly-dolly. Mrs. Wright likes me, and she'll let me have them on friendship. Won't our Jana love a dilly-dolly, Paw?" William's eyes danced. "And it'll be small enough that she can take it along with her when we move."

"I'll talk to the real estate agent while we're in town." Richard started toward the stucco shack with the water, his mind already making its way through the pinyons and junipers and cedars, past the sprinkling of ponderosa pines, looking ahead to his beloved valley where dearth was a stranger.

CHAPTER NINE

The Strange Encounter

Deana took a few tentative steps, clinging to the bedspread. Then she plopped down, cushioned by her diaper.

"Look at you!" cheered Anna. "You'll soon be walking! And won't Daddy be surprised?"

It had been a long morning, filled with pangs of loneliness. A brief shower of rain, an antidote to the stifling heat, had come—and had gone—and the sun was back on its throne.

With the passing of days, Anna's devouring impatience had muted to boredom. Her thoughts all had one center: the boundless happiness she'd have in her new home in the New Mexico Territory. Time crept like a snail, much too slowly now, as if life had throttled to a halt. She yearned for a change. Surely Jason would come this week. . . .

"Mary Butler says we forge our own chains," she said aloud to the baby as if the child understood every word, "and this room is giving me a locked-in feeling. Silly, jumpy little worries are eating away at me. I think I have a case of cabin fever. Let's go down to the lobby and wait for our nice newspaper boy."

Go was probably the only word that Deana comprehended, and she held up her arms to Anna. "Go," she repeated.

The first floor of the hotel was littered with people. She was glad; she didn't want to appear a solitary figure without friends or family. She mingled, blended, and exchanged good mornings with several of the women, enduring remarks about the weather.

Most of the men clustered in little knots of conversation. Someone mentioned the county fair, and she supposed that affair had brought the throng to town. It reminded her of the mob who camped on the banks of the South Canadian River awaiting the Oklahoma land run. She hoped the restaurant had ordered enough food to feed everybody.

"Ah, we meet again!" A male voice spoke in a parody of courtesy. "Mrs. Lewis, I believe?"

Anna's heart beat like a captive bird's while her eyes swept in a slow half circle until she located the speaker. Lucius, the carriage driver, leered at her with an evil glimmer. His face flushed until it seemed as if the fires of iniquity flamed through his cheeks and cracked his lips. When his mouth twisted in a derisive smile, she caught a whiff of his breath, a smell she associated with Lesley Horn.

"So your husband hasn't arrived yet, madam? *I* think that you haven't a husband! Or else he has abandoned you—"

Anna lifted her chin so as not to betray how his familiarity disturbed her. "He is on his way here at this minute!" She hoped it was the truth.

"I like your vinegar, honey. You're a spunky one. You'll be well taken care of even without that fictitious man of yours. Your beauty manages to make itself obvious in spite of that baggy dress and severe bun of hair." His hunting eyes held their own secrets.

Afraid that her legs would fold under her, Anna turned her back on him and quickly weaved her way through the crowd. Trembling, she dropped into a chair beside an old woman with a gray crest of matted hair and a curved beak of a nose. The papery face reminded Anna of a wrinkled turnip. Her skin sagged in all the wrong places. She hummed a doleful minor tune.

Anna smiled at her.

"My dear!" the beggarly elder spoke in a high, honking voice. "It is so nice to have your company. And what a lovely baby!" She fixed her watery eyes on Anna as if she had the power of life or death on every soul who met her gaze. "Everything passes by too fast to see, doesn't it? Life goes roaring on just when we think we have it fixed in a frame and can look at it. See all these people? We must all stop now and then to catch a true glimpse of things, don't you think?"

Anna gave a nervous laugh. "Actually, I wish time would pass a bit faster. My husband is on his way here and I can hardly wait!" Again she hoped that what she said was true.

"Eh?" The spare and charmless woman's ears did not serve her well.

Instead of shouting louder, Anna moved closer. "I'm hurrying the time for my husband to arrive."

"Ah, the rush-rush of youth! But tell me, is your

husband a good man?"

A joyous answer boomed up. "Oh, yes! He's the best man in the world!"

"Some go all through the forest looking for a straight stick and have to take a crooked one in the end."

"Jason is wonderful!"

"Well, I say a husband is one package you never can tell about until you get it home and get the wrapping off. Then you know if you got a bargain or not. But say, I'll wager a pretty lass like you tumbled into a dozen pens of puppy love!"

"No," Anna said. "I never had a beau before Jason."

"Not many get their beau straight as an arrow." She shook with a convulsive laugh. "But with some, it just comes natural."

Anna thought of all she'd gained and had yet to gain, her mind skittering about. She'd gotten a bargain all right. She had wed a noble man with truth inside himself. He was the straight one, Lesley the crooked.

Deana tried to squirm from her grasp, and she put out her hand to retrieve her. She heard a hiss of caught breath and a choked cry in the old woman's throat.

"Your hand!" the woman uttered with horror, pointing.

Anna looked down at her hand. "What . . . what's wrong with my hand?"

"I see death in your future! In your palm!"

Anna stiffened. "I'm . . . I'm not superstitious.

A chuckle came from the old blue lips. "*Everybody* is superstitious, my dear. That's how I make my living!"

"I believe in . . . God."

"So do I. He has granted me a special gift of hindsight, foresight, and insight. Do you remember what Johann

Strauss sang in dying?" She reverted to the humming of her melancholy song, this time even more off key. "No matter how beautifully the sun shines, sometimes it must set."

From the corner of her eye, Anna saw Lucius edging toward the door. Blackness flickered and menaced around the arc of her vision. She was caught between a desire to run and a shame of doing so. If only Jason would arrive right now!

"I could even tell you about your past."

"No, I . . ."

She lowered her sparrow voice. "I'll say it quietly so nobody else can hear."

"I'd better take the baby up for her nap."

"Wait! This is not your firstborn baby. You have a sinful past, and your mother has your other child. Your mother is ill. You must go to her at once even though she lives many miles away. Your husband is jealous, and if he finds out that you have a son, he will leave you. And sad that would be because you married a *wealthy* man." She stared at Deana's handsome hand-smocked dress, a gift from Mary. "You married your husband for his money. But then, money is life's essence." She grinned. "Without money life is too thin for a fork and too thick for a spoon. Your husband will become more wealthy yet, for wealth begets wealth, you know. Now that telling will cost you a quarter."

Anna shook her head with a kindly refusal. "I hope you don't have to depend on your 'sights' for a living because I'm afraid they are far from correct this time. Indeed, you missed your conclusions farther than you hit them!"

Suddenly the old lady's expression was like an empty house. Her confidence was vanquished and ran gibbering away. "Well, it was a good try for a meal."

"You might be wise to try something else."

On her face Anna saw the furrow of old tears. "I used to think that as I grew older, I'd become young again each spring," she said. "'Come spring,' I'd say, 'I'll be strong. I'll plant flowers, tie up pepper vines, gather sunflower seeds, and put them in store for winter.' How fragile a thing life is, yet how stubborn when it decides to cling!" Her voice seemed curiously separate from her body. "I decided to try to fool people by pretending I could see into the future. What can one do when one's earning power is gone? It's a frightsome thing, child. I'm nigh on to ninety, and the rest of my family has done gone on. I have no one to earn my bread and I refuse to beg!" She sagged like a collapsed scarecrow. "And now you've called my bluff!"

"Do you need money for food?"

The aged woman gave a pinched nod. "I've been trying to cut back. Do you remember the story of the donkey whose master trained it to eat less and less? Just when he got it down to nothing and was congratulating himself, it up and died. I can feel the last bit of fluid ebbing out of me like grains of sand sliding one by one through the narrow neck of a bottle. I'm hoping that those grains of sand are not lost but that they're accumulating somewhere in a more lasting pile."

This poor soul has no flesh left to wear away, Anna thought. Her whole tapestry of life was threadbare. Her high-mileage clothes dripped from her shoulders. Anna reached into her pocket and gave the pitiful woman a dollar.

She looked at the silver piece with a dreamy awe, then gave a toothless laugh. "Why child, that will keep me till I die! I . . . I didn't *beg*, did I? I promised my Abe that I'd never be guilty of a beg—"

"No, you didn't beg."

"Now child, don't give no howdy-do to what I said about a death in your future. I tell *everybody* that. That's my trick. It gets their attention, then they're ready to pay for happier news." She pulled at her bushy eyebrows. "Really, I am the one who is facing the end, and I'm always trying to push the last chapter off on somebody else! What is old age and death but the turning of a page that will soon be gone? At least the grim reaper won't catch me by surprise. Nosiree!"

It was a strange encounter, but it had rid Anna of Lucius. When she looked around, he was nowhere in sight.

CHAPTER TEN

Chance Meeting

The slanting rays of the morning sun had awakened dozens of windowpanes. As Anna stood looking out, her thoughts dipped this way and that like the gray pigeons she watched pinwheeling in the sky. She had been here almost a month. It seemed more like a year. Where was Jason?

She'd counted her money and found that she still had plenty. Her harsh economics had left enough to take them on to their land. And if they ran short, lean times didn't frighten her.

The squawk of the fire wagon's horn tore at the air, angry and close. She could hear the excited shout of people below. A foreboding, beginning as a small cloud on the horizon of her mind, grew into a terrible storm, almost suffocating her. What if the hotel was on fire? She and Deana would be trapped on the second floor with no way of escape! A cramp of anguish seized her. "Oh, God," she prayed, "save us!" Her lungs turned to kettles about to boil.

Fear leaped into angry life. She grabbed up Deana and

her suitcase and ran down the stairs, taking them two at a time, her hair loose and flowing.

The registrar shoved himself from his chair. He was a dark lump of a man, but Anna didn't waste time in taking his measure. "Is something wrong, missus?" he asked. "Are you leaving in such a hurry?"

"No, I . . . I . . ." Fear loosened its grip. "Is the . . . the hotel on fire?"

"At the first scent of fire here, madam, we would have all our patrons out before they could smell the smoke. We guarantee round-the-clock protection."

It had been a trick of her mind, of course, conjured up from solitude. Her actions had been taken over by her aloneness. She felt like a child lost in a nightmare. Everything was tottering about her or had, perhaps, already come to ruin without her knowledge.

"I . . . I thought . . . that is, I was afraid . . ." The sentence died away, unfinished.

"I'm sorry that the fire wagon startled you. We who are accustomed to life in town think nothing of it. But of course, you must not be used to the city. It's all one big Saturday afternoon, and a coffin is as likely to be full of whiskey as it is a corpse.

"I would suggest that you get out and move about rather than cloister yourself in your room. The hours will brighten with diversion. If not for yourself, then do it for your child. She needs sunshine."

"Oh. Oh, yes, I'm sure . . . she does." She turned and fled back up the stairs, feeling childish and stupid for her unfounded panic. Sometimes she felt older than her eighteen years, but just now she felt much younger.

She twisted her hair into a coil at the nape of her

neck, moving briskly with decision. She must get out, get Deana out. The man was right. Fresh air would do them both good, and perhaps her appetite would improve. She didn't want to be pale and pasty when Jason came or have him notice that her clothes didn't fit as well as they did at Mary's.

She looked up and down the street, wondering which way to go. The icehouse, crouched halfway down the block to her left, was doing a bustling business. Drivers of wagons, coming and going, wrapped big blocks of ice in burlap. She turned to her right, walking aimlessly, passing stores with their mingled odors: spices, candles, and coffee beans. She could hear the mutter of voices and the clinking of items into sacks, the sounds of living.

In a display window was a jar marked "Soap"; it was filled with shredded flakes. Through the open door she saw a young sales girl cutting from a bolt of calico, scissors in hand. Farther down the street was a small library. She stepped inside to find rows of calf-bound books and volumes of Wordsworth's poetry.

"Are you new here?" the librarian asked. She wore a dark blue gown with a high frill at her throat and a lace cap over her hair. She was the epitome of efficiency.

"Yes and no. I . . . I used to live south of Lubbock, but I've married now."

"You are welcome to check out any of the books you'd like. There's a limit of four books to be returned in thirty days. Reading broadens the mind."

"My husband is on his way, and we will be moving on to the New Mexico Territory. He'll likely be here . . . tomorrow."

"How long have you been waiting?"

"Almost a month. I'm staying at the hotel. I didn't know there was a library near."

"And you could have been enjoying our books all this time! A good book is like an old friend, comforting and companionable. I find that books help me let out my intellectual hemlines."

"I've been purchasing a newspaper every day."

Anna wandered on down the street and then back again. She heard the faint sound of the train whistle in the distance and figured the station must be at least a mile away. Her thoughts drifted, swam in idle inconsequence in the creamy warmth of the day. She was enjoying the outing.

"Anna!" A familiar sound, dimly remembered against the boundaries of time, reached her. She whirled about so quickly that her skirts stayed twisted about her legs. Was it—?

It was William—taller, thinner and with a voice gone deeper into his throat. The boy who only yesterday was all arms and legs was becoming a man. She remembered him as a kid not shoe-broken. Children were like lanky colts, sticks and knobs and eyes and a shaggy mane, and suddenly they grew up.

"Willy!" Her mind was going faster than her tongue, a part of it thawing out. She must not let him know that she had married Jason. Jason had said they would break the good news together. "You've grown!"

"Remember you've been gone most nigh a year, Anna. I'm almost twelve now. And I've been helping Paw make decisions—"

"How is—?" Anna started to say Maw, but couldn't. "How is your mother?"

"She's not doing well at all. Her flesh is dropping off fast, and she has a pesky cough. She needs a tonic, but we don't have the money to give the doctor. Paw won't credit. You know we have a baby now, don't you?"

"You mean, your maw has a baby?"

"Yes."

"A boy or a girl?"

"A girl, and she's a dandy. I take care of her lots for Maw. I love her so that I'd . . . I'd give my life for her! She's most nigh as big as yours now. Is that the same sickly baby that was at our house during the sandstorm last year? Maw was sure she wouldn't survive."

"This is the same baby. She looks spanking fine now, doesn't she? She's trying to walk. I named her Deana for her mother. You know, don't you, Willy, that I'm not your real sister?"

"I know. Paw told me. But it makes no matter to me. In my heart, you are my sister."

"Of course. But since I left, I learned that Deana's mother was my real sister. That makes Deana especially dear to me."

"Were you on your way back . . . to us? Maw said you wouldn't be back, but me and Paw were sure hoping you would."

"No, I'm staying here at the hotel waiting for my husband."

"So you got married after all?"

"Yes."

"Me and Paw didn't want you to marry Lesley Horn. But mayhap he's changed."

Anna passed over William's comment and hurried on. "We're going to my land in the New Mexico Territory."

"You'll come by to see our baby won't you?"

"Oh, yes, we'll come by."

William rattled the sack he held in his hand. "I've just been to Mrs. Wright's to get some spools to make my baby sister a dilly-dolly. I'll make one for your baby, too, if you'd like. Mrs. Wright gave me extra spools. I'll have the dolly ready for your Deana when you come by." He reached out to touch Deana's hand, and she responded with a gurgle of delight. "Willy will make you a dilly-dolly, too, sweetie."

"That would be lovely, Willy. Deana would like that."

"Paw says we gotta do something soon. He's seeing a real estate agent about putting our land on the market. We'd thought on going back to your land where they once lived, but we didn't reckon on Lesley Horn going back there, too. Paw don't cotton to Lesley's ways. I don't think they would get along. So I don't know what we'll do now."

Anna reached into her pocket and brought out a five-dollar bill. "I want you to take this, Willy, and get your maw some medicine."

Williams' eyes bulged. Anna supposed he had never seen a bill so large. "That's way too much, Anna. Paw wouldn't want me to take Lesley's money, anyhow." He kept his hands behind him as if trying to resist the temptation to take the bill.

"It isn't Lesley's, it's mine. And I have plenty. I insist that you take it. My husband will have more when he gets here. Your family took care of me for more than fifteen years, and I owe them a great deal more than this."

William took it reverently. "It's a miracle," he whispered. "A bigger miracle than you know. Thanks."

"And tell your Paw not to make any rash decisions

until he talks to Jason."

There was a moment of awful silence and sweat began to grease Williams' face. His lips tightened. "I guess you haven't heard, Anna, but Jason is dead. He was killed. Paw got the word—"

"*Jason . . . dead . . . ?*" As the black pain welled up from the depths of Anna's being, she stood stunned, dry-eyed, and disbelieving, too stupefied to force order into her thoughts. There was nothing to say to ease the unendurable moment, and she bit off a scream of protest. She could not find the words she needed if she searched for a lifetime.

"It was like I died myself when we got the news, Anna. I depended on Jason for so many things! Not something to eat, but for how to act and how to say things and what to feel about things that happened. Like he taught me not to hate by never hating no matter how anybody treated him. When I stood beside Jason, I felt *tall*.

"Remember when the scorpion stung Jason? He never cried even when it puffed up and felt like fire. Well, before that I baby-cried easy if I got a little hurt, but after that I never did. I wanted to be brave like my brother. I used to see my reflection in the watering trough and wish that my face was made the way his was. . . ."

Anna didn't remember when William left. She stood blindly on the boardwalk, oblivious to the passersby finding her an obstacle in their way. Her world had splintered. The great tidal wave of grief and despair swelled and broke. Then it gradually went back to sea, leaving her cold . . . and without an anchor.

CHAPTER ELEVEN

A Time for Trust

Anna lay on the bed, rigid and tense, not knowing that she had finally gone to sleep. She had felt the sting of death and now she must face the scourge of her empty days. As with any shock, it wasn't the moment of revelation that was worse, but a time hours later when the mind's anesthesia wore off.

Just now, in her stunned bereavement, she thought that her heart would break. It was too much to bear, the current too strong to withstand. She had been snatched by a great wave, whipped about, half drowned, then tossed up on a barren shore.

For the first time in her life, she must make her own decisions. She was cut off from her past. Hope for the future no longer bloomed in her head; it hung like a tattered rag, weighted with lead. She had expected beauty; it had turned to ashes. Her dream had been too perfect to last.

Where had Jason been killed? When? How? She had failed to ask the questions that now crashed in upon her. William hadn't offered much information. In her blind instinct of self-preservation, a part of her had shielded itself against the intense rays of the moment. She knew now that she hadn't wanted to ask, to know, to hear. Jason's death, so unexpected, was almost impossible to come to terms with.

Pulling herself to the edge of the bed, she sat motionless in the grip of incredulity. Had Jason rescued her from Lesley Horn only to be snatched away?

Jason was everything to her . . . and he had died somewhere between here and there. She would never know where his grave was. Within her was something that would never cease to ache. *Jason, if only you could have told me goodbye!*

The scent of day came into the room, and Deana awoke with a restless whimper. Anna supposed the child sensed her trouble. She picked her up and held her to her breast. She began to rock back and forth. "Poor baby," she crooned. "You'll never know the love of a daddy. Jason will just be a name to you. We don't even have a picture of him for a memory!"

The sympathy caused the child to start crying.

"There, there. Don't cry."

I will continue one foot in front of the other for you. Her sister's child was her only focus now. The baby must be hungry; she had to be fed even though Anna was heavy eyed and weary.

In the tearoom, the waiter tried to make light conversation, but Anna couldn't smile. *He doesn't understand. I should be wearing a black dress, but I don't have one and can scarcely afford to spend any of the money I have left for clothing. It's a good thing I gave Willy the money for Corine before he told me about Jason, or I might not have had the courage to part with such a vast amount.* She ordered nothing but strong coffee for herself.

"I'll bring extra cream, ma'am," the attendant said. "There's nothing worse than being scrawny."

There's nothing worse than being a widow at eighteen, her thoughts responded, the sense of loss a yawning hole in her heart. Death was a thief. *But I'm glad I had him. . . .*

She knew that she would never be really complete without Jason, yet she had to go on living. She still had one purpose for existence: Deana. She could thank God for that. She pulled the child closer to her. "We'll find a way," she whispered.

A young couple came into the restaurant for breakfast. They smiled and talked, sharing a camaraderie she would never know again. She sat staring, her mind closed against an empty future that she could not, would not think about. *Dreams die hard.* Mary said that when she talked about her childlessness.

Feeling a peculiar weightlessness in her stomach, Anna hurried Deana through her meal, longing for the sanctuary of her room. Her head ached as if her skull were opening and shutting. She couldn't be sick in the eating area!

Back in her room again, her eyes fell upon the family Bible. *What time I am afraid, I will trust . . .* She could hear Jason quoting it now. Did she doubt that God could handle her burden of grief? She knelt beside the spider rocker to pray. Then suddenly, overwhelmingly, she felt a Presence in the room. It wasn't visible, but it was enough. This Presence would help her with her unknown future.

She couldn't see into the tomorrows, but He could! It was as if some sealed section of her mind were blasted open and all the possibilities lay open before her.

Should she go back to Mary? Mary would say that time heals all things. But that simply wasn't true. There were things that time couldn't heal. Mary would gladly take her and Deana and nurture them until her dying day. She would, in fact, spoil them, think for them, shield them from life's injustices.

But could Anna be happy with her own and Deana's destiny in the hands of another, no matter how capable those hands? No. It was her own obligation to provide a home for her sister's baby, and she felt a desperation to have a place where she and the child could *belong*, could live independently.

Going to the Lewises' was certainly out of the question. There wouldn't be room for them in Corine's home . . . or in her heart.

Every day in the hotel was taking more of her precious resources. She would need to move out to a cheaper facility and look for a job at once. She had never worked. The life that lay before her was fraught with every possibility of failure. It would demand physical and mental strength—and an inner vision. She would have to find the thread that sewed one day to the next to weave a stable life for herself and Deana.

One thing she knew. She couldn't thrive on leftovers from her past. They were nothing but pieces. If she could pick them up, where would she take them? Death had come with such swift and cruel finality. There was nothing before her, and behind only unbending shapes. Her world whirled around and around, spinning into a dark, narrowing funnel.

Midafternoon, Anna heard a timid knock at her door. She had been crying and hated for anyone to see her red-ringed eyes. When the knocking persisted, she called out, "Who is it?"

"It's William. There were some letters for you General Delivery at the post office. The postmaster asked if I would bring them to you. They're backed to 'Anna Lewis' and the sender's name is missing. I don't know who they're from. I'll slide them under your door if you'd like."

"Please, Willy. Thanks. They're probably from Mrs. Butler, a friend of mine. I'd invite you in, but Deana is asleep, and I have a terrible headache."

"I'll see you when you and Mr. Horn come by, Anna."

Anna opened one of the letters. It was from Jason, and after reading the first paragraph, she couldn't bear any more of the sweet sentiments. She folded it and put it back into its envelope. Maybe there would come a day when she could bear to read the letters, but not yet. She slid them into her suitcase beside the land deed.

The land deed. She still had the land, and according to Jason, there had once been a home place there. It might be liveable. That would beat paying rent. But how would she make a living in such an isolated place? Nothing would succeed on wishes alone. It took strength and will.

How did Maw and Paw make a living? she asked herself. *I could make a living like they did.*

She looked at her white hands. *These hands can plant and plow and harvest. These hands can feed chickens and milk cows. These hands can bake and quilt and churn.* Jason said it was a mild climate. Surely there would be roots and berries and nuts for food. All she had was her own genius—and God—but that was enough.

By morning, after a sleepless night of grappling with problems that slid away like slippery minnows, she had made her decision. She would go to her land. She'd go at once. There was no time to waste on self-pity. Already it seemed half a lifetime since she had heard of Jason's death. She had a short, sweet golden age, one brief span of dream days, to look back on. That would make the real days bearable. And hopefully, grief would dim with the smudging of time. She would take the carcass of her dead dream to her own land for interment so that she could have her own memorial days. There she would grow old, but Jason would remain forever young.

Then someday life on earth would burn through the perishable into the eternal—and she and Jason would be together again. . . .

Her decision impelled her to action.

CHAPTER TWELVE

Corine's Reaction

"The tombstone made Jason's grave not so . . . bare, didn't it, Paw?"

"It did. For all of time, people who visit the cemetery will know that the man who is buried there had a family, a brother who loved him. A hundred years from now, it will still be standing. Rocks never wear out."

"Jason left me with a lot to live up to, Paw. I'm going to try to be a man worthy of such a brother. As I see it, real men are mighty scarce nowadays, and since Jason got knocked out of the game, I'll have to step up and take his place. I want to be as good a big brother to Jana—as brave and honest—as Jason was to me."

They'd spent the night in the wagon, and Richard checked the harnesses for the journey across the chalky flat as if welcoming the niggling irritation of common things. He shifted the box of supplies from one side to the other for the third time. Now he put it as close to the hard board seat as he could get it, his hands caressing the crate. The boy looked past his father's eyes into the private place of pain and regret, and he changed the subject.

"The money from Anna was truly a miracle, wasn't it, Paw?"

"That it was, Willy. Your meeting up with her was no happenstance. I wish I could have seen her for myself. I've been lonelying for her worse since Jason died. I needed to tell her that we are only accepting the money as a loan—"

"I don't think she'll take a repay, Paw. She said her husband would bring her by to see us on their way to their land; you can tell her then."

"Mayhap Lesley Horn has grown up, or mayhap my estimation of him was out of joint. Neither Jason nor myself much liked him. He was cruel to his animals, and Jason caught a smell of spirits on his breath. But I'm willing to let bygones be bygones if he'll make Anna a good husband. I hope that she is happy."

"Anna seemed awfully happy to me. She said she was waiting for Lesley to come for her. I didn't ask her if he was somewhere in town, but I expect he was. She had his baby with her. They are staying at the hotel."

"You told her about Jason?"

"Yes, sir. After that she wasn't happy anymore. I could see that the news set her back."

"She was partial to Jason above us all."

William's face was a brown study. "I was wondering, Paw. What'll we do about going back to Anna's land? I mean, we couldn't go now, could we? You thought Anna would live out her life in the Oklahoma Territory, and she didn't. What will that do to our plan?"

"I couldn't be beholden to Lesley Horn. Even if he's different than Jason and I thought, I couldn't ask to live on his property."

"It's Anna's property."

"It will be Lesley's now."

"But you put our place up for sale today! What will we do? We'll have *no place at all?*"

"The land man was out; he won't be back for several days. So our little plot isn't on the market yet. I was sick at heart until . . . until you came with the money from Anna."

"And we'll have enough to carry us until the real estate agent gets back?"

"Or longer. The tonic cost less than I figured on. I had four dollars and four bits left. I spent four dollars on food and supplies and kept the four bits for emergencies. It makes a fellow feel good to have something put back."

"Maw ought to perk up when she sees all these staples."

"I even got her a kit of mackerel and some rice as a surprise. Won't she like that?"

"Did you ever tell her that you were going to sell the place and go back to New Mexico?"

"No. I knew she would protest, and I was afraid I'd weaken in my decision, especially with her sickly."

Summer's dying breath blew dry and the evening air was sweet. It combed through William's earlobe-length snarl of untamed hair. The smell of the desert's spicy unknown scents and its thundery silences soothed the ache of William's spirit. Tumbleweeds and sand were all he had ever known, and he found beauty and healing in the wide-flung and mysterious prairie.

The sun lost its streamers of red, gold and purple, and by the time they reached the adobe hut, the sky was alive with stars that looked like silver cutouts pasted on a black sky.

Corine had a lamp burning for them. "I couldn't sleep," she fretted. "My stomach was too empty."

"No more empty stomachs, Corine," Richard said. "We've brought supplies—and plenty."

"Did you credit for a few meals, Richard?"

"No, Corine. We had a miracle. Willy and I made a prayer to our God on the way to Lubbock, and He heard us. We asked Him to provide us with a way to buy food for you and Jana. And He did."

"He did it . . . for *me?*"

"For you and Jana."

"Then . . . I *believe*. I vowed that if He'd do somethin' just for me, I would believe. I'll stick to my word. But how . . . how did you—" A fit of coughing brought an ill-bred interruption to her question.

"Willy brought me five dollars."

"*Five dollars?* Surely, Richard, you didn't pledge away the horse and the wagon for a morsel of bread?"

"No, Willy ran across Anna, and she—"

"*Anna?* Is Anna back?"

"She and her husband are in town, just passing through. She asked after your welfare, and when she learned that you had a plaguesome cough, she gave Willy the money to get you a tonic from the doctor. There was enough left for food, too. I even brought you some mackerel."

Her eyes, muddy and listless, regained some of their old flame. "Mackerel! Oh, Richard, it's been so long . . ."

"And rice, too, Maw!"

Her fingers fumbled with a broken button on her dress. "I don't . . . understand. Why should Anna care if I cough or not? I . . . sent her away."

"She said she owed you more than she could ever repay," William said.

"And she has God's love in her heart, Corine," offered Richard. "God's love makes one forgive."

"I . . . I want to see Anna." Desperation echoed in Corine's voice. "I *must* see her. Will you take me to town tomorrow, Richard? I . . . I have a powerful lot of apologies to make to Anna. They weren't leavin' today, were they, Willy?"

"I think not. Anna said she had a headache when I—"

"Lesley is bringing her by here on his way to New Mexico, Corine. You'll have an opportunity to say anything you wish to her then."

Corine looked from Richard to William. "Lesley Horn is bringing Anna by *here*?"

"That's what she said, Maw."

"Then Esther Horn was right. Lesley's heart is good. Lesley wasn't lazy or a bibber. It was pure grief that made him act th' way he did. He was sorrowin' for his lost wife. Esther *said* he had a big, lovin' heart underneath. She knew her son better than any of us did."

"I hope so, Corine."

"Could you tell if Anna was happy, Richard?"

"I didn't see her."

"She was glowing happy, Maw," William said. "And remember the scrawny baby that you thought wouldn't live? She's roly-poly and pink cheeked now just like our Jana. Her name is Deana. Anna mothers her just right. The only thing—when I mentioned Jason dying, Anna went sad. She felt by Jason like I did."

"Yes, she was heart-closer to Jason than she was to me or any of the rest of us. But that wouldn't be hard, since he was th' one that saved her from th' Indians. Even if she doesn't remember it in her mind, her spirit remembers it."

"She knows about her own family now, Maw. She knows we're not her kinfolks."

"How did she learn?"

"Lesley Horn's wife that died was Anna's own sister. Anna found her sister's journal or something—"

"Well, if that isn't the queerest thing! We thought her sister had been captured and killed, too. But how do you suppose Anna got so much money so soon?"

"The way she and the baby girl were dressed, I'd say she struck it rich in the Oklahoma Territory. She could thumb her nose at us poor folks, but she didn't. She was worried about you, Maw."

"I feel like I can get well now."

"Did you see Anna more than once, Willy?" Richard asked.

"No, I didn't actually see her the second time. Anna got a bunch of letters come General Delivery from somebody. They didn't have a name on the backing. She hadn't picked them up, so the postmaster asked me if I would see that she got them. She said they probably came from a lady friend she met up in Oklahoma. She said she had a headache and the baby was asleep, so I pushed the letters under the door. There were about eight of them in all."

"How long has she been here? To get that many letters, I mean."

"I think she just got here. The letters were all addressed to Anna *Lewis*. I'm supposing she met up with the lady before she married, and the lady didn't know she had changed names."

"It would seem that Anna *planned* on coming back,"

mused Richard, "since she gave the woman her maiden name and a Lubbock address."

"Girls are changeable, Richard. She might've planned on returning to us, then decided to get married. Every girl wants to wed the first chance she gets."

Richard turned toward the door. "I'd best unload now. We wouldn't want any night creatures to help themselves to the wonderful food that God has supplied."

"Has Jana been asleep long, Maw?" William cast his eyes toward the baby's pallet.

"Since th' evenin's twilight."

"I got the spools from Mrs. Wright. When she learned why I wanted them, she gave me a whole sack full. I got enough to make *two* dilly-dollies. I'll make one for Jana and one for Anna's baby, too. I'll make them just alike!"

CHAPTER THIRTEEN

The Journey's Onset

Stagecoach schedules were posted on the wall in the hotel's entry. At the first sounds of morning, Anna lifted the still sleeping Deana into her arms and went to check the timetable. She knew she must go south, but just where her land lay, she didn't know. She needed to find someone who had a map or knew the location of the land.

"Pardon me," she said to an anonymous-looking man who peered at the chart himself. "Do you happen to know what coach I should take to get me to the New Mexico Territory?"

"Depends on what part you're going to, ma'am," he said. His face might have been chiseled from marble, or some cheaper stone. "You could go south, west, or southwest. It's all bad country. What is your destination?"

"I . . . I don't know."

"Then I would suggest that you find out where you are going before you depart." He chewed his mustache with his lower teeth, squinting at the schedule again.

Anna went back to her room and pulled the deed from the suitcase. There were no directions with it, but the county was listed as Dona Ana. That would help. Businessmen who sold land were knowledgeable about geography. She would go there; the office was in the next block.

When she arrived at the real estate agent's office, a note on the door said that he would not be back for several days. Now what should she do?

The library! The kind lady who sat with the books might be able to assist her. Surely she would have an atlas or a globe. Anna hurried to the library but found that it didn't open until nine o'clock.

She wouldn't waste time. She'd feed Deana and then begin packing for the journey. Without Mary's stash of crackers and dried fruit, the portmanteau would be lighter than when she came.

She was standing at the library door when it opened. With an extreme sense of duty, the librarian welcomed her. "And how may I help you?" she asked.

"I need to know . . . how to get to my land."

"We can get the information you need!" She swung the door wide. "Please do come on in!" She unrolled a huge map sketched on canvas and began her search.

The symbols and lines and markings made no sense to Anna.

"Here! Here is the county you're looking for. It is midway in the New Mexico Territory, backed up against the Rio Grande River, near a place called Fairacres. You'll likely have to go to El Paso, then catch a ride up to Las Cruces and on over from there. Let's see. That is at least five hundred miles from here."

And a thousand miles from Mary Butler. "Do you know anything about stagecoaches?" Anna asked.

"Oh, yes! My father used to run the Butterfield Route when I was a little girl. But that has been discontinued. It was a scenic and dangerous trail. Papa had many stories to tell. I don't think there's anything but a four-horse line that takes mail now. And it doesn't even make meal stops."

"Oh, then how—?"

"Is your husband interested in becoming a stage driver?"

"No, I . . . I wanted to *ride* the stage. You see, I . . . I just received word day before yesterday that my husband lost his life . . . on his way here to me." As the words left her mouth, Anna realized she walked the delicate line of hysteria that threatened to spill over on the wrong side.

"You got the news after you left the library that day?"

"Yes." Tears sprang in spite of her fight.

"Oh, my dear little mother! And left with a baby! Sit down here! I had no idea—" She steered Anna to a chair. "And now you have no one. I will take you home with me!"

"No, I really must get on to my land while . . . while I still have the resources."

"And you want to go by *coach?*"

"Well, yes, I—"

"Oh, but you mustn't think of going by stagecoach! Stagecoaches have hard springs, and they can only travel fifty miles a *day*. That would be a ten-day trip to El Paso, then a couple of days of weary miles on to your land. And those horrible things stop at the old stage stations every twenty miles. The food, if there is any, isn't edible."

"But I—" If she took the train, that would mean a shuttle ride to the depot with Lucius, and Anna shrank from that thought. She couldn't walk the long distance to the depot with Deana and her suitcase. At the memory of the carriage driver, her stomach tied in knots.

"You *must* take the train to El Paso, then get a coach from there. A train can have you to the border in two days even with rail trouble."

Anna's mind tumbled back to the Pullman berth where she and Deana slept fitfully, jolted awake every time the steam whistle screamed into the countryside. "I know it's faster, but—"

"Really dear, I think that a train will be your *only* means of transportation. I doubt that you have a choice."

"Then I—"

"But please stay with me for a few days. Your emotions are too raw, and you're in no condition to travel alone. I'm afraid that the shock of the tragedy hasn't hit you yet."

"I'm sorry, but I must go. I would only be delaying the inevitable. Sooner or later, I have to make it on my own. Right now, I have the funds to relocate."

"How old are you?"

"Eighteen."

"That's too young to take a child and go into the wilderness. I would suggest that you give yourself time here in the city where there are *people*. We help each other here. You might work for a few months. I can help with the baby. I fear that you are going to an isolated place."

"I must not grow dependent on others."

"How will you earn a living?"

"I'll survive the same way my mother and father survived: off the land."

"Oh, but they lived in a different generation. What if—?"

"I cannot consider what-ifs. This is what my husband would want me to do."

"Then may I help you to the train station in my buggy? I'll get someone to stand in for me while I'm gone."

"Oh, would you please?" Anna's heart opened in gratitude. That would solve the problem with Lucius, the boorish driver. "I'll go for my baggage."

When Anna stopped by the desk of the hotel to turn in her key, the manager taunted her. "So your husband has come for you, huh?" He turned his head from side to side as if looking for the invisible mate.

Anna started to say something, then her mouth snapped shut like an angry clam. She felt far from shore, being swept relentlessly toward her destiny. Her future was of no concern to the hostelier.

"And when will you and *your husband* be returning, Mrs. Lewis?"

"We will not be returning, sir."

He had one leg crossed over the other: calm, confident, waiting for her own words to trap her. His eyes were flinty; he was enjoying her discomfort.

"And if anyone should call for you *or your husband*, Mrs. Lewis, where shall I tell them that you have hied yourself off to?" The question seemed an accusation.

Anna's face was white and set. The muscles in her shoulders tightened. If indeed she had a reservoir of strength, it had sprung a leak. "Tell them," she said steadily, "that we have gone to our marvelous land—and anyone of significance to me will know where that is." He needn't know that the "we" was she and her sister's child.

"May I have a forwarding address in case mail comes for you?"

"We have no address yet."

There was an early afternoon train. The librarian took Anna's trembling hand in parting. "There are many ways of facing grief, dear," she said. "Some rail and storm against it. Some turn doggedly to anything that might drown the terrible pain of loss. These are very sad to see. Then there are those who deliberately shut themselves off from life because they feel life has betrayed them. They lock up their hearts and hide the key. They lack the gift of tears. These are the most destitute of all. But there's the saint's way: 'Thy will be done.' I pray that you find it."

The ticket to El Paso took such a bite from Anna's savings that she experienced a nibble of fear. But once on the swaying train, she sat still and let the hours pass, thinking of the bad and the good and wondering why bad things happened to good people. Why were the Jasons taken and the Lesleys left to corrupt the earth?

It wasn't until late evening that she remembered her promise to Willy—the promise that she would come to see the baby sister of whom he was so proud. It was just as well, she decided. Corine and Richard would never have to know that she was their daughter-in-law.

The shade of night pulled down around the locomotive that snaked its way across the sage-sprinkled miles. Out the window, the moon rode like a golden curl of hair upon the shoulder of a cloud.

The long journey had started.

CHAPTER FOURTEEN

Mixed Emotions

Anna's legs wobbled when she stepped off the train. Her body felt disjointed, each member unstable. She and Deana were covered with enough soot to blacken a tub of bath water.

Since leaving Byers Bend in July, Anna had learned many things. She knew how to summon her own carriage and give the driver instructions. She'd learned that carrying her own luggage saved tipping. Now she hailed a buggy to take her to the stage station for her next leg of the journey.

"Actual', you won't have to go clear to Las Cruces," the man behind the litter of stage schedules told her. "That will cost extry. You can hump off at Mesilla and get a trap on out toward Fairacres. Ciphered rough in my head, I'd say it's less'n five mile on from there. Ever traveled this line, missy?"

"No, sir."

"We allow thirty pounds of free luggage with extry at six bits a pound. We got a perfect safe record. We don't hire no show-off drivers. If they smart up, we show 'em off to another line. The back seat of th' coach is always th' best; it faces rightward. It's not often we transport lone women here so clost to th' border. We'll be honored to have you bump along with us. And never fear. Th' trip is through settled country; farms and fields and orchards and some fine timber along the mighty Rio Grande. One good bone-shaking day'll get you there. There'll be some slow trudges uphill and some careful shuffles down. Coach departs at eight o'clock."

"This evening?"

"Oh, no'm. In th' morning. No stage till tomorry."

That meant finding a place to lodge for the night among these short and dark-skinned people. "Could you recommend a boardinghouse nearby?"

The man gave his thumb an impolite jerk. "Crost th' street. It's cheap. Fifty cents a day with meals throwed in—or throwed up. Can't say I'd use th' word recommend, but staying there would spare you some shuffling. You look so wagged out you could probably sleep on a sack of soup bones."

"Thank you."

The accommodations were by no means luxurious, but now Anna had to pinch every penny if she hoped to get settled on her land. The room was small, musty and cramped. The smoky lamp that hung from the ceiling had a sinister way of increasing instead of brightening the gloom.

An old spool bed with a packed, straw-filled mattress and a stiff pillow took up most of the space. Undisturbed dirt lurked in all the corners and the smell of pipe smoke made her queasy. Before she put out the light, she examined the bed for crawlers.

Her body yearned for sleep, but her mind refused it. Her back ached, then her shoulders, then her neck. She tossed restlessly trying to find a comfortable spot, waiting for the emotions that churned through her to finally wear her out.

Waking with dawn, Anna compared the journey with her own life—it first moved over level ground, then stumbled over rocky passes to emerge into this strange and unfamiliar landscape. Would she ever find the strength to mend the holes torn in her life?

Breakfast was a terrible conglomerate of stale bread, boiled meat, chili peppers and greasy cabbage. Anna had to ask for milk for Deana, and the results of her request was a watery whey.

An angry argument broke out in the dining area over statehood for New Mexico. "We've had enough population to qualify as a state since 1850!" bellowed a man not tall enough to carry his overweight. "Idaho and Wyoming have been in the Union almost ten years now, and New Mexico has a larger population than either of those states!"

"Is it Washington or Santa Fe holding out?" The second man had a thin upper lip and tricky eyes.

A third man topped with hair as black as washed coal, waved his arms and jabbered something that Anna could not understand.

"You can hear anything!" the first man exploded. Imagining he had a table in front of him, he banged his fist on his own knee, hurt himself and calmed down. "We're one of the last frontiers, and many big landholders are afraid statehood would mean higher taxes."

"Big landholders, bah! I hate them!"

Anna listened with trepidation. She supposed she

would be considered a landholder.

"Purely selfish, to be sure. I say shoot them all!" His voice was cold enough to make a polar bear shiver.

They're talking about me! Anna fell prey to primitive fears.

"Some say the whole matter is manipulated by a few politicians in Santa Fe. Others say the Union isn't eager to have us, either. Somebody up in Washington was quoted as saying they didn't want any more states until they got Kansas civilized."

"What it amounts to is we're in the United States but not of the United States."

"Si. Si." The black-haired man's piercing eyes snapped.

Anna looked about, wondering what there was to see, half expecting him to point toward her, identifying her as the enemy. But the man strode out, his heels striking hard.

"Why couldn't we just all get together and vote ourselves in by simple majority?"

"Alvin, surely you are not so naive! Voting in New Mexico is a joke. Have you never heard of stuffing the ballot box?"

"No. What is that?"

"There are stories floating around about ranchers voting all their sheep when an issue is in doubt."

The angry voices, the hate, the wild gestures all coalesced to terrify Anna. What had she gotten herself into? Her soul cried to be rid of problems. She had imagined a land of timelessness, a place where the monster of fear was chained in its lair, a place where she could begin life anew and find peace.

She fled from the room.

CHAPTER FIFTEEN

Interim

Unmeasured hours passed over Anna, and the day wore on. It was late when she reached Mesilla.

Dark would catch her before she got to her land, so she inquired about lodging and was directed to the home of a Dutch woman named Nagel. It seemed the lady already had enough of her own without boarders, but Mrs. Nagel said merrily, "We don't turn nobody off!" Then the good woman invited Anna to "spare her bonnet" and to sit her grip "there in yon corner a'ready."

Much of the woman's speech took some deciphering. She asked Anna where she "scared from" and then exclaimed, "Now think! So off fur. It's a wonder a body'd be contented to live that off fur a'ready." They had settled in the New Mexico Territory years ago, she said, when their name was "Getznagel yet a'ready." But they had "shortenered" it to "just clear Nagel."

Mrs. Nagel introduced Anna to her children. Of the oldest, a pock-faced boy named Jake, she said, "Till December Jake'll a'ready be seventeen. And he's never sit up with a girl on Sundays a'ready." Jake blushed. Anna supposed that "Sunday sitting" meant courting.

"Then this one here is Leonainie. She ain't never got her tongue with her when there's guests a'ready. Her paw said she shain't have a Sunday sitter till she'd *eighteen*, but her paw ain't." Anna guessed the girl to be about fourteen. She was beautiful now, in an unfinished way, but when the richness of maturity came to her, she would be startling.

Anna counted four children between Leonainie and the baby, who seemed a tiny creature of another clay.

"Do you feel for some vittles?" Mrs. Nagel asked.

Anna hesitated, feeling confused.

"We're havin' fried mush fur supper. We got cracklin' mush and plain mush. It wonders me if you like it a'ready?"

"Yes, I like mush," Anna said. "Any kind." It smelled good, and she felt faint.

"I took up guesting when my husband turned off to heaven a'ready and left me unmoneyed. I had to stop guesting onct," rambled Mrs. Nagel. "I got it so in my leg. But the doctor helped me a heap a'ready. Will you let here long with us? Outside taking guests, I butter and milk and cheese. That daily breads us."

"I'll be going to my . . . my own home tomorrow."

"An' won't you be glad to get home a'ready?"

"Yes, I will."

"We had the strangest long guest onct a'ready from Pencil-vania. He didn't addict to no bad habits, but he washed his feet as much as onct a week, and in the wintertime a'ready! It wondered me that he didn't die of fistulics. He could say two words with the selfsame meaning. I say more'n one's squandery. Jake asked him pine-blank was he a drummer. He said no, he was a prof . . . prof . . ."

"Professor?"

"That's his calling. Funny thing a'ready. I had cucumbers. He said he couldn't eat cucumbers in the evening with impunity. I told him these here is with *vinegar*. He laughed a'ready, but I spied no laughedness in it."

The Nagel boys were shooed to a pallet in the parlor floor after supper so that Anna might have a room to herself. "Oh, I must not misput you!" she objected.

"A pallet don't make nuthin' with them boys!" discounted the good-natured mother. "They're used to it all their lives a'ready. It's like play fun."

Anna's bed was turned down to welcome her dragging body, and although her feet felt very dusty from the trip, she didn't ask for water to wash them. She didn't want to be a tale on Mrs. Nagel's tongue for the next boarder.

On the wall of her room, pages torn from an almanac offered a variety of messages for occupants. "Sharper than a serpent's tooth is to have a thankless child," one read. Another said, "Hearts, like fruit, ripen sweetest with the frost." And a third, "Pure happiness lasts only two seconds and a half."

During her brief snatches of sleep, Anna's mind hummed with senseless dreams. But she could bear up to anything, she reminded herself, because tomorrow night she'd be "home."

The next morning, Jake offered to take Anna to "the town's heart." He had to take butter to one of his customers, and he said it wouldn't be out of his way. "Their butter's all anymore," he said.

"You mean they're *out* of butter?" Anna asked.

"*Out* of the butter? Och! I hope nobody'd fall *in* the

113

butter a'ready!" The thought seemed to horrify the boy.

"Do you deliver every day, Jake?"

"I have to work behind Fridays or Saturdays."

"Mayhap you could deliver milk to me?"

"It wonders me how near you are."

"My home is in the country."

"It costs too expensive to go fur. Och! And the butter would cream again a'ready. But I'll wrap up and leave you have a gallon of richy milk fur your home first a'ready today."

He said he'd wait while she got the information that she needed about the land.

Anna showed the deeds to a Mr. Roper and asked if he could give her directions to the home place.

"Indeed I can, Miss Anna," he said. "I knew your father long before you were born. There was never a better man who walked about in shoe leather. You bear quite a favor to him, I might say. He couldn't have disclaimed you! I remember the day you put in your appearance on earth. Your father wanted to name you Donna Anna, his Americanized version of our county here: Dona Ana. That's pronounced Dough-na Ah-na. But your mother wanted to name you Michelle after herself, so they named you Anna Michelle. I'm the one who recorded your birth. I'll never forget your father coming in that day, shouting, 'Mr. Roper, I got me another fine girl!'

"Nobody was more taken aback by that Indian massacre than me and my Judith. And to think, you're the only one who survived."

"My sister survived, too. This is her baby. She chanced upon a wagon train going through to California, and they took her along with them. Mother had pinned this land

114

deed to her petticoats, and that's how I happen to have it."

"Well, well. So your sister is alive also?"

"Not now, sir. Unfortunately, she died last year. I have taken her child to rear."

"And what of the child's father?"

"He didn't want her."

"And you've come back to settle here?"

"I have."

"You've a prime piece of property out there, Anna—a fruitful valley with its head resting on the lap of a hillside and its feet dangling in the river. It is a most beautiful vista. Someone came through just last week wanting to buy it. But some hunch told me that you would return when you were of age. Do you go by the Lewis name?"

"I married the Lewises' son, Jason. Then I . . . I lost him to an accident . . . just recently. I'm . . . I'm a widow." This was the first time she'd said it aloud. The words were like rocks thrown into a canyon—one had to wait for the crashes below.

"Please accept my sympathy, Anna. I realize that grief of this magnitude can't be shared. Everyone carries it alone, his own way. . . ."

"To find someone who knew my family helps."

"Now about the property. Mr. Fleming over at the bank will need to talk with you before you settle in. He has been keeping up the taxes on the place all these years."

"Is the house still . . . liveable?"

"Oh, very! Nothing has changed much since your folks . . . left. Mr. Fleming and myself have sort of taken turns seeing after the place since Mr. Lewis left. We've tried to contact you over the years, but could not locate you."

"I knew nothing of my history. I didn't know that I was an Elliott or that I had land."

"The Lewis family didn't tell you?"

"No, I found my sister's diary."

"I see."

"Can you draw me a map to get to the place?"

"Yes. It isn't hard to find, but it is much too far to walk. I could take you, but then you would be alone without transportation. You must think about purchasing a horse."

"Could I buy one . . . reasonably?"

"Go down to the livery stable and tell old man Tomlin that I said to give a lady a fair shake with a gentle bronc."

"Are there . . . roots and plants on my land that can be used for food?"

"The soil here is most productive, a veritable Garden of Eden! *Anything* will grow. But you want to take care when picking plants at random. We have a dangerous plant that grows in New Mexico. It's called peyote, and it is a narcotic. The leaves are light blue, it has pink flowers, and its root is carrot-shaped. Eating it causes mental derangement."

"I'll . . . I'll watch out for it."

With a slip of paper bearing directions, Anna had Jake take her to the bank to see Mr. Fleming. Jake seemed to be enjoying the service he was rendering.

Anna's mind was in a state of agitation. If Mr. Fleming had paid the taxes all these years, she must owe him a staggering sum. How would she ever clear the debt and keep her land? Finding that Mr. Fleming was not in, Anna found herself relieved not to have to face him yet.

At the stables, Mr. Tomlin said he'd sell her his best horse for "a sawbuck or two fins."

"A sawbuck?" Anna's mind was blank.

"A ten or two fives."

Anna dismissed Jake with a thank you to his mother.

"And don't ferget us a'ready," called Jake. "When I'm oldered, I might like to sit up with you Sundays." Red dyed his neck as he urged the team to a frantic departure.

Mr. Tomlin picked a horse for Anna. "This one's as strong as an ox and as tame as a lamb," he affirmed. "*And* pretty as a picture." He led a beautiful chestnut mare with a white blaze face to Anna. "Her name is Caballocita. That means the sweet little horse."

For ten dollars, the old gentleman threw in the bridle and saddle. It took the last of Anna's money. She had only a few cents left.

CHAPTER SIXTEEN

The Arrival

August blurred into September, and autumn sent out its first message with cool nights. Everything took on a renewed vitality. Everything, that is, except Jason Lewis. There was nothing like carrying a horror around in one's heart—and having it grow.

"You're not eating, Jason," dogged Mary Butler. "Have another biscuit."

"I . . . I'm not hungry. I thought surely I'd hear from Anna today!" His voice revealed the cruel torment of a spirit burdened with unrequited questions. "I just can't understand it. I've written to her at least twice a week for these two months. And *nothing*! I don't even know if she ever reached Lubbock!"

"Did she have any identification on her, Jason?"

"Yes, she had the family Bible and the land deed."

"Then we would have heard by now if anything had happened to her. No news is good news my maw always said."

"But I asked her in my letters to write!"

That night Mary talked with her husband, Theodore.

119

"It's unfair to keep the boy any longer. He is only staying out of a sense of duty to you. Pay him and send him to his wife and baby! Have pity on the poor man. Can't you see that he is dying from within?"

"He hasn't complained once, Mary."

"He wouldn't."

The next morning, Theodore Butler paid Jason half a year's wages for the two months of work. "I'm firing you," he grinned. "Mary thinks your wife needs you worse than I do."

"I can't take this wage," Jason protested. "It's too much."

"You were more valuable to me than any other three workers I could have hired," insisted Theodore. "I want to help you and Anna get a start on your land. Mary worries that I've kept you too long. No amount of money can compensate for the separation from your family."

Jason, on a horse as impatient as himself, boiled across the plains, fitted to the saddle. He moved as one with the stallion, riding hard and long.

Worry badgered his mind like a canker sore. No word from Anna was *not* good news. If all was well—if she had gotten his letters—she would have responded. Had Lesley Horn trailed her? Jason set his jaw hard. It was the first time that wrenching thought had assaulted him.

He didn't count his traveling days; they ran together in a haze. When a need for sleep forced him to stop, he slept with troubled dreams, his heart a void, hollowed out with an unknown dread. One night, camped above a nice spring that ran down a ravine, he dreamed that she was beside him. When he reached for her, she slid into the shadows. After that, sleep was elusive. Every river, every

canyon, every crazy-angled arroyo seemed bent on sepa-
rating him from his destination—from the one he loved
more than he loved life itself.

When at last the city limits of Lubbock came into
view, Jason's apprehension mounted. It seemed he had
lived a dozen lifetimes since he left early in April. He felt
something that none of his five senses could identify. It
brought a strange, flat sensation into his chest.

He had a four-day stubble of beard. He stopped at a
windmill to wash the trail dust from his face, change into
a clean shirt and tame his hat-mussed hair. Vanity wasn't
in his vocabulary, but his reflection in the cattle tank
assured him that the quick grooming had helped.

He turned up Main Street and went directly to the
hotel. "In what room may I find Anna Lewis, please?" he
asked the clerk.

"She doesn't board here anymore." The man behind
the counter clipped the words and went back to his
accounts in the ledger book.

"When did she leave?"

"That is against my policy to disclose, sir."

Jason saw that any information he got would be
parceled out narrowly; he would have to be persistent to
learn anything at all. He decided that the man disliked
women as a matter of principle.

"Do you know where she went from here?"

"No."

"Did she . . . did she leave any message when she
left?"

"She said that she *and her husband* were going to
their *marvelous* land." The mocking tone was accompa-
nied by a malicious smile.

"*Her husband?*"

"Yes." His voice didn't budge an inch.

"He was . . . with her?"

"*I* think she didn't even have a husband! He certainly never showed his sideburns around this hotel!" The meaning of his acrimonious words were unmistakable.

Like an animal, Jason's flesh gathered and bunched at the scent of scandal. "She *does* have a husband, and *I* am her husband!"

Jason's outburst shattered the man's set-jawed poise. He shrugged. "The only person I ever saw with her was the child. How should I know?"

"I don't know why she left before I arrived, but I plan to find out—"

"Maybe she gave up on you."

"I wrote to her twice a week. She knew my plans." Jason tried to ignore the insulting remarks. He refused to let blind rage control him.

"Don't blame me for your domestic embroilments, sir! That's all women are good for if you ask me."

"I didn't ask you. And I'll take the room my wife stayed in while she was here, if you please."

"How many nights?"

"One."

The clerk made the transaction with cool indifference. "Good luck," he jeered.

After tethering his horse outside, Jason went to the second floor room. *She stayed here. She slept here.* He could still smell the faint trace of lavender soap. *But now she is gone.*

The thoughts that visited him were filled with blanks, pieces to a puzzle that didn't fit. Apparently, she had left quite abruptly. Was she running from someone? His mind was on a treadmill that wouldn't stop.

As he set his valise against the wall, he noticed a scrap of paper almost buried under the edge of the rug. When he dug it out, he found that it was one of his own letters to Anna. He supposed she had dropped it. It had never been opened.

The mystery was too much for his mind. A bud of confusion bloomed into regret. Whatever had happened to Anna lay to his own charge. She had begged him not to send her on ahead. Her voice echoed in his memory yet. He had sent her away against her wishes even as his mother had done a year ago. He thought he had done it for her own good, but now he realized he had been thoughtless.

But why had Anna left before he arrived? There was no meanness, no pettiness in her. She would have done nothing out of vengeance, out of frustration—or even out of impatience. She was not an ill-tempered girl. The only thing that could have impelled her was *fear*. If given time, Jason decided, he might dislodge the rock that covered the root of the problem.

The arduous hours of travel came to collect their dues as he lay face down across the bed. He melted into sleep, his body welcoming the relief of a bed as dusk deepened. When he awoke, the black of night was dusted with gray, and daylight climbed up the sky in the east. It was a clear morning, but the dark shadows of uncertainty were still with him.

He sat up jerkily like a wooden rule unfolding. *She probably went to Maw and Paw's!* The thought slipped whole and cool into his mind. *She may have run short of money. She knew we would need a good wagon and team for the trip. If she hit on a bargain, she skimped herself tight of funds. That's why she couldn't stay longer at the hotel. Why didn't I think of that before?* The tightness in his chest gradually began to give way. He was certain that he would find her, safe and happy, at his parents' home. He gave a liberating laugh, castigating himself for his needless concern.

Since he was in town, he told himself, he should check the mail for his family and save Paw a trip in. Maw sometimes got a catalogue, and now and then Richard ordered something that needed picking up.

The postmaster handed him a bundle of letters—all addressed to Anna Lewis. He counted them.

It had been a month since Anna had picked up her mail.

CHAPTER SEVENTEEN

Willy's Disclosure

Across the treeless distance, the speck of adobe hut took shape.

A prickling, like a grass bur, scratched at Jason's mind. Before him lay the heartbreaking tale of slow erosion of his father's farming on this parched prairie. Few could survive the sheer grit that life here demanded. How differently things might have been for his family elsewhere! The tragedies and struggles would surely have been less harsh in a kinder climate. Failure was so close to the marrow that it left one's naked soul scantily clad.

The fight of the past sixteen years had certainly left its injuries. *Some wounds, if left unattended, never heal.* He had read that somewhere.

Jack rabbits nibbled on the sparse grasses, keeping a safe distance with cocked ears as Jason thundered by. One fearless jack, as big as a puppy, refused to move, and the horse kicked sand over it. A lizard sitting on a stone disappeared in a flash of flame.

There were no fences, no houses, no people. The vermilion and magenta blossoms of the cactus plants lay open to the power of the September heat. They'd endured the dry summer and never wilted. Nothing had changed— or would ever change. Progress found no reason to encroach on this land.

Home. It had been a hard cot of a bed, a black iron cookstove, and a splintery washstand weathered to a sickly gray. But it was his home no longer. He was now a family man with a wife and baby to support, and the sooner they settled in another slice of the country, the better. He and Anna would need to go on right away. Tomorrow wouldn't be any too soon. If Anna hadn't already done so, he'd buy a covered wagon and a pair of stocky horses. . . .

The stallion recognized his familiar turf and whickered. In his eagerness to see Anna, Jason left the animal ground tied and made for the house at a run.

His mother stood at the stove, preparing a meal that combined breakfast and dinner. A baby played about the floor, a dark-haired, dark-eyed baby. If this was Deana, she had changed completely in the eight weeks since he had seen her. He looked about for Anna.

Corine Lewis tottered and would have fallen if Jason had not caught her. Her face twisted, and her mouth formed words soundlessly. A croak, the audible part of her stifled scream, reached the surface of her lips. "Nooooo . . ."

"Maw! Maw! What is wrong? You are ill!"

"Am . . . am I dead, too?"

"No, Maw, you just started to fall. I'm sure you're not dying—"

"But you are dead! And I'm . . . where you are." She pulled back from him.

Poor Maw. Had she taken leave of her senses while he was gone? The desert made equal demands on all, men or women. Had the awful desolation finally broken her mind? Where was Anna?

"Maw, I'm not dead. I'm right here talking to you. Here, touch me. I'm your son, Jason."

Her eyes were wild. "Where have you been and why have you come for me?"

"Didn't Anna tell you?"

"Anna? Anna who?"

"Listen, Maw. When I left in April, I told Joshua, the smithy's son, to tell Paw that I had gone to the Oklahoma Territory to see about Anna. I told her to write to us General Delivery if everything was well with her, and when no letter came in all those months, I suspected that she needed me. I got a newspaper that gave the land run date and found that I didn't have time to come back here if I expected to get there and find her before the crowd fanned out across the land. That's where I went—"

"But you were shot . . . in the tavern."

"No, no, Maw. I wasn't shot. There *was* a young man shot the day I left, but I never learned who he was. And you thought that I—oh, Maw, I'm so sorry! I thought Joshua would tell you."

She seemed to reach for his words cautiously, as though afraid they'd leave. "He . . . he didn't tell us nothing—except that he was sorry for the accident." Her words were flat to match everything else about her. Her face was flat. Her forehead was flat. Her cheeks dropped in flat planes to a mouth that was straight and wide.

Jason smiled down at the baby. "Deana has changed so much! She seems . . . smaller. But where is Anna?"

"I . . . I haven't seen Anna since she left here last year. Willy saw her in town about a month ago. He said that

127

she . . . she married Lesley Horn."

Married Lesley Horn? It couldn't be; it wasn't possible.

"Then Anna isn't here." Disappointment and torment gripped his heart like a vise. He was as confused as one awakened too suddenly from sleep. He hadn't considered that she might *not* be here. He was so certain that she would be. A sick hollowness accosted him.

"And this here is our own baby, Jason. Your baby sister."

Jason didn't hear her. "Where is Willy, Maw?" If William had seen Anna, he had to talk to him at once.

"Out at the windmill a-talkin' with your Paw. We gotta do somethin', Jason. We're a-starvin' to death."

Jason stumbled out, his head in a spin. "Willy!" he called. *"Willy!"*

William's face turned ashen, and Richard's eyes were expressionless, like water over a stone. "Paw," William managed a thin whisper. "It's a man that looks exactly like Jason!"

"It *is* your son, Paw," Jason responded. "I've already talked to Maw, and she said there had been a mistake. She said you thought I had been killed—"

"And you warn't, Jason?"

"I'm alive and well, Paw."

"Jason!" William made a dive for Jason and wrapped his arms around his brother's body. "I done put a headstone on your grave! I'll have to go and take it off!"

"By all means!"

"Oh, Jason!" The boy's voice rose in a burst of joy fervent enough to wipe out all the past anguish. "I can't believe it's really you! It's like you've been resurrected."

"Willy," Jason pressed, "Maw said you saw Anna in town."

"Yes, it was about a month ago. She was staying at the hotel waiting for her husband to come and take her to their land. She said he was due to arrive any day. She promised me that Lesley Horn would bring her by to see us."

"*Lesley Horn?*"

"Her *husband*. She got married while she was gone, Jason. That was the plans when she left here, I think."

"She told you that she was married to *Lesley Horn*? She said his name?"

William looked confused. "Well, now that you mention it, I don't believe she called his name outright. I called his name, though, and she didn't say anything. I knew—"

She didn't want to reveal our secret, Jason reasoned. *She was waiting for me to get here like I asked her. But she's not at the hotel now. What happened to her?*

"Tell me everything you remember, Willy. Every little detail. Don't leave anything out. It is terribly important—"

"Has something happened to Anna?"

"I don't know."

"Me and Paw went to town with some big troubles on our mind, and I met up with Anna on Main Street in front of the hotel. She was surprised at how grown up I was. First off, she asked about Maw, and when I told her that Maw had been ailing and we hadn't the money for a tonic, Anna gave me a five-dollar bill. I didn't want to take it, thinking it might be Lesley's, but she said it didn't belong to Lesley Horn, it belonged to *her* and that she had plenty more.

"That was mine and Paw's miracle we'd prayed about. Paw said we'd pay her back someday. We had prayed for some way to—"

"And then Anna told you she was waiting for her husband?"

"Yes. And then I told her about our baby—"

"Our *baby*?"

"We got a baby right after you left, Jason. And she's the dearest thing! Paw named her Jana for you and Anna. Didn't you see her in the house?"

"Yes, but I didn't know—"

"I'd gotten some spools from Mrs. Wright at the millinery to make a dilly-dolly for our Jana, and I told Anna that I would make one for her baby, too. She explained to me that the baby was really her own sister's child. I told her that I would have the dilly-dolly ready when they came by on the way to their land. And I've looked for them every day, but they haven't showed up yet."

"Was Anna . . . well?"

"Oh, yes—that is, when I first saw her she was. She seemed wondrous happy . . . and she looked beautiful. She had on a pretty dress and had her hair all up in curls. I guess she prettied up for her husband to come. But when I told her about you dying, her sad quiet was worser than any loud cry I ever heard. She was still standing on the sidewalk lost-like when I left."

"Anna thinks I'm *dead*?"

"We all did! I told her that Paw had got word that you had been killed."

"But I wrote her . . ." he stopped. "And that's the last time you saw her, Willy?"

"I didn't see her again, but I talked to her through her room door later in the day. The postmaster asked me to take some mail to her. The letters were all addressed to

130

Anna *Lewis* and the sender's name wasn't listed. When I knocked on her door, she said she had a fierce headache and her baby was asleep, so I pushed the letters under the door and said I'd see her when she came by. Whoever wrote the letters didn't know that she was married and had a new name."

Pictures dropped in and out of Jason's mind, and he was drowned in the impact of the sudden revelation in such vivid color. Anna, thinking him dead, left for her property in New Mexico to try to make it on her own rather than return to the Lewis household where she would not have the welcome of a daughter—or a daughter-in-law. His family thought that Anna was Lesley Horn's wife. They had no suspicion of his impromptu marriage to Anna.

He must go to her immediately and spare her more anguish. His dear, suffering darling! She had had a full measure of heartaches in her short life.

Jason closed his eyes tightly and tried to think. Where would he begin to untangle the web of circumstances that today had woven for him?

Chapter Eighteen

The Land

On the loping horse with Deana pulled tightly against her, Anna wrestled with demons of doubt. How would she ever be able to come up with enough commodities to make life supportable for herself and the child? Even uncomplicated lives devoted entirely to survival depended on *food*.

Could a baby survive without milk? She had the one gallon that Jake had given her. It could be watered down and made to last several days. That is, if she could keep it cool so that it wouldn't spoil. Then what?

And there was the problem of the property taxes. How would she ever—?

What Anna saw when she reached her land made her forget her grim, practical list of impossibilities and hold her breath. She had never seen any place more wild or more beautiful. She was filled with peace at the sight of her valley, endless in its variety. It reminded her of a jewel in its setting.

The more she saw, the more it pleased her. She knew at that moment that she must find a way to keep it—that not only would she accept the land, but the land would accept her. She would prize every tree, every dew-sequined blade of grass. Her past was here; her future was here. If she could root herself here like a perennial, spring would come to renew her.

The house was almost hidden in a grove of squatty trees. Her first priority was to see if the structure was immediately habitable. It didn't look a ruin at all; no one had disturbed it in all these years.

The spreading stone house had a low-pitched roof, its shingles silvered with time. Here was a house that offered more than protection from wind and rain. Here was a house where one's heart, as well as one's body, might find a safe shelter. When she fitted the key into the lock and the door swung open on rusty, neglected hinges, she felt a familiar warmth as if she were returning to a place she had known all her life. "Oh, Deana, it is a *grand* house!" she sighed.

The front door led into a parlor, larger than any room Anna had ever seen, and more magnificent. In one corner sat a square pianola. Already her fingers itched to touch it. In a vision, she could see her mother sitting on the round, three-footed stool.

The stuffed chairs all had antimacassar-covered backs and arms that matched. She suspected they were a product of her mother's needle. On the wall, six or eight photographs in narrow oval frames formed another oval, all equidistant from the largest that occupied the center not only of the group but of the wall. Someone had a symmetrical eye for decorating.

Anna tasted something from the distant past, some dust-covered memory, and knew that the featured picture in the middle was her mother. She stood in awe, looking into her mother's face, and could almost feel herself being charged by her energy and strength. Her mother had been delicately pretty, fine-boned with upswept hair, her eyes transfused with tenderness.

She imagined her father tramping in and throwing himself on the horsehair sofa with dirt from the fields clinging to his clothes while feeling no remorse or fear of reprimand. There were photos of her brothers and one of her sister, an older version of Deana.

Anna was anxious to see the rest of the house and wandered into the kitchen. It was as her mother had left it: orderly and neat. In the center of the big room, with space to spare, stood a table with a checkered cloth. On a wooden platter, a loaf of dried bread and shriveled cheese had deteriorated to near nothing.

The room looked "lived in." Kindling and logs were stacked in the tinderbox by the cookstove, and a jar of matches sat on the warming shelf. A row of stone jars with lids lined the cabinet. They bore labels: flour, sugar, cornmeal, salt, tea. Anna unscrewed the lid of each jar and every one was full. There was also coffee and a can of leavening. Here were enough supplies to keep them from hunger until she could get her wits about her!

An 1871 calendar graced the wall, scribbled with little handwritten reminders. The letters sat straight and even-headed, shedding more light on her mother's personality. Anna had wanted everything in order all her life; Corine's haphazard ways had troubled her. Now she understood why. She had inherited some of her mother's characteristics.

Water was piped into the kitchen from an artesian

well. Her father had been sensitive to her mother's needs and wanted the best for her. Her father was a man like her Jason had been.

Deana had fallen asleep in Anna's arms, and Anna sought a bed to lay her on. The bedrooms were identifiable by the clothes in the armoires. The girls' clothing hung in the room with the smaller bed, and Anna placed Deana on the smallest trundle. It was where Jason had found her. . . .

In the room introduced by boys' paraphernalia stood a great bed with columns topped by a bug catcher. Hand-drawn sketches brightened the walls. At least one of them had artistic ability.

She took in her parents' bedroom by degrees. There was a chiffonier filled with frothy undergarments. She would go through that later.

On the cheerful patchwork quit stitched in a flower-garden pattern lay her mother's diary. Embossed in gold on the front was the name Naomi Michelle Elliott along with an inscription: "Dream the Old Dreams Over." Anna broke down and wept. Dare she trust her emotions to allow her to read her mother's deepest thoughts?

With trembling fingers, she picked up the journal. "This strange and virgin country demands a compelling loyalty," her mother had written. "Reuben says that one loves it or one hates it. There is no in-between. Our tenant's wife, Corine Lewis, does not love it. I love it, for I have learned where to look for its beauty."

On another page was written: "One's own belongings, humble or great, are worthy of being cherished, guarded, kept whole. I hope that I may pass on to my children and grandchildren some of the treasures left to me. Grandmother's silver thimble. Mother's teapot. Aunt Eva's shoe spoon. I will put them in the trunk so they will not be lost or damaged."

On some pages, Naomi Elliott spilled her heart. "The greatest of all tragedies would be to leave this world without having known life had a purpose, was a preparation, had a meaning. Each of us must concentrate on the eternal, which tends to make the temporary look trivial. I'm grateful that Reuben, who could preach with his Bible shut, is leading each of his children to God. He is a noble husband."

Anna thought her mother's analogies beautiful. In one entry, she wrote of the moon "like a silver coin stuck to the windowpane," and in another she described a willow tree "blowing in the wind like freshly washed hair."

A few books sat on a square table near the bed. They were arranged in cubical piles in perfect order. There was a volume of James Whitcomb Riley's "love-lyrics for fragrant retrospection." Someday she would read it, Anna decided, when the sharp edges of her sorrow had worn away.

An ornate teapot commanded her attention. She lifted it, finding it very heavy. Removing the dainty lid, she found five silver pieces inside. Five dollars! That would buy gallons and gallons of milk for Deana!

The trunk proved to be the most sentimental journey of the day. Her mother's Gainsborough hat, tilted up at one side with a jaunty air, had a knot of red roses sewn under the upturned brim. Anna tried it on and examined her reflection in the mirror. If only Jason could see her now!

Then Anna saw it . . . the garment started . . . the knitting needles stuck in the yarn. . . . She picked it up. What was her mother making? An unfinished baby sweater. Then Anna knew. When Naomi Elliott left the earth, she took with her an unborn child.

Anna put the aborted project back and closed the lid.

CHAPTER NINETEEN

Plans

At breakfast, Jason surveyed the skimpy table, ashamed to let his eyes count the pancakes, but unable to resist it. William ate with more appetite than usual. Jason recalled his mother's words when he arrived: "Jason, we're a-starvin'."

"What kind of jelly is this, Maw?" he asked.

"Prickly pear. Your paw likes it."

"Tastes like figs," Richard said.

Jason gazed with horror into the black depths of failure yawning at his father's feet. He could hardly bear it. Richard's eyes were dull with worry. Something must be done. Jason felt sandwiched between a need to run to Anna and a responsibility to his suffering parents. If he abandoned them, what would become of them?

"We're mighty glad you've come home, Jason," Richard said. "We were trying to figure on some plan for ourselves. There ain't much left for us on this drought-proned land. Earnings here make thin slices when divided among so many needs. But now that you are home to help me make the living, we'll figure something . . ."

Jason's abashed look told Richard too much too soon. Richard's sentence skidded to a stop, trailing a wake of silence. "What is it, Jason? Don't you plan to stay here with us?"

There was no exit but honesty. He would neither lie nor evade. Jason's mind turned mental cartwheels. He and Anna had planned to make their announcement together.

"No, I . . . I have a home of my own now."

"You staked you a place in Oklahoma?"

A little humor might rescue the tense situation. "Now hold your whiskers or they'll blow off, Paw. I got me a wife. I'm a *married* man now."

"A *married* man?" Richard's voice went flat, cold-tinged. "Then where is your wife? Why didn't you bring her along to know her to us?"

"She's . . . why, you already know her!"

"How could I when we never met?"

"I went to the Oklahoma Territory and . . . and married Anna."

"Anna? *Our* Anna?"

Diamonds of sweat stood on Corine's dark face. She could empty her face of expression at will.

"Yes."

"Aw-*right!*" cheered William. "Only I wish I could have been the lucky one!"

"You married your own *sister*, Jason?" blurted Richard.

"I knew for all these years that I would marry Anna someday," confessed Jason.

"I knowed it, too," Corine put in.

"You planned it when you left?" Richard asked.

"No," Jason said. "But when I found her, I had no

140

choice. You see, Lesley Horn was planning to marry her, and I had to beat him to the draw."

"I'm surprised he didn't challenge you."

"He found somebody else."

"Reckon why Anna didn't tell me it was *you* she married, Jason?" quizzed William.

"I asked her not to. We were coming together—"

"What about the . . . the baby?"

"Leslie didn't want to be bothered with her. He gave her to Anna. Lesley was married to Anna's sister the first time, and Deana is Anna's niece."

"Willy told us."

"You have your own family now, Jason." Richard kept his voice controlled as if the physical effort to do so was almost beyond him. "You mustn't be bothered about us."

"But you are my family, too. What are you planning to do the winter, Paw?"

"Got no plans, Jason. None. Can't sell our last and only cow. That would be suicide. But I guess just staying here is suicide. Guess we'll just be like the widow woman in the Bible—use up our two sticks and die." His melancholy matched Jason's distress. It seemed that death roosted in the room.

A hovering intention suddenly crystallized. Jason wished he could discuss his decision with Anna, but that wasn't possible. She would understand his position as a son.

"Paw, why don't you load up and move back to New Mexico with Anna and me? The cabin will likely still be there, and if it isn't, we'll build another one."

"Anna wouldn't want me near, th' way I ill-treated her," Corine spoke up. Her hands knotted together in a nervous gesture.

"Anna hasn't a bad-tempered bone in her anywhere, Maw," Jason reminded. "She'll be generous-hearted about it. If I could ask her today in person, she'd be agreeable. I'm sure she would."

Richard, picking up on the crack in Corine's armor, got behind the idea and pushed to get it rolling. "I could help you with the farming, Jason. It's a big place. You'll need someone, and I already know the way the land crops. Course I wouldn't expect no wage, just a-plenty to eat would be a grave for my worries!"

William's eyes shone with excitement. "Me and Paw talked on returning to New Mexico once, but after I saw Anna and we thought she had married Lesley Horn, we dropped it, knowing we would lock horns with a Horn!" He gave an adolescent laugh. "And mayhap I could even go to school and learn elocution and be a writer or a speaker or a . . . a governor!"

"But, Richard," complained Corine. "I'd be leaving all these graves . . ."

Richard let her fuss, knowing that grumbling was her only defense before surrender. She absorbed ideas slowly, like a trickle of water through a crack.

"But you must give equal time to your first-buried," reminded William. "That's only fair. Now if it was *me* underneath that dirt, I'd want you to come back to me."

It was the right thing to say to sway Corine.

"It would take a couple of weeks for us to ready-up for the trip," Richard said.

"I'll need to go to town today and send Anna a telegram—"

"They likely don't have telegraph service away out there, Jason."

142

"Then I'll post her a letter. I don't want her to grieve a minute longer than she has to."

"To be sure. We don't want her heart bleeding. We need to go in to town anyhow and talk to the land-selling man about this place. We'll go tomorrow. If I could just get enough to make the move—"

"Paw, I don't want to see you give this place away," Jason said. "I have enough to pay your way to New Mexico. In fact, all of us could take the train tomorrow and be there in three days."

"Oh no, Jason," objected Corine. "I couldn't leave my nice furnishings here. That iron stove belonged to my own mammy. An' there's the quilt box Richard made for me an' th' iron bedstead. Even my old tin washtub's gotta go along. An' th' wooden churn."

"And I wouldn't want to part with my horses, Jason," Richard said. "They're like part of the family. We couldn't get everything on the train. No, we'll have to wagon it all through."

"Then you'll need a new wagon, Paw."

"Like as not I will."

"How long will it take you to make it by road?"

"Took us seven weeks a-coming. We might beat that some goin' back, though. There's some rough ground between here and there and a couple of wide rivers."

Seven weeks? Could he wait seven more weeks to see Anna? They'd had such a short time together—

"Just help me get the land on the market, Jason, and you can go on ahead of us. One person can travel faster than a whole family."

"I think I'll go by train myself, Paw. That'll get me to Anna more quickly, and I can be getting your house ready against when you come."

"That's a good idea, Jason." Corine joined the planning with a brief light in her eyes while William flung himself about in ecstasies of juvenile enthusiasm.

"We'll *all* be together again—and with the babies, too," hurrahed William. "Once I thought I'd never smile again, but I think when we all get moved, I'll never be able to *quit* smiling." He squatted on the floor where Jana sat on a braided rug. "And *you*, my little princess, can take along your dilly-dolly that Willy made for you when we go bye-bye."

She picked up the doll by its spool leg and gave it a shake. "Bye-bye," she echoed.

"Jason," Corine's words were slow and measured. "I'm worried about the baby on such a long, hard trip. There's rivers to ford an' insects an' stormy weather. Could you take Jana on th' train with you? Would Anna mind keepin' her for a few days until we can get there?"

"Anna wouldn't mind, Maw. She loves babies. And I'll take Willy along, too."

"I might need Willy, Jason," Richard said. "He's most nigh a grown man now. Look at those muscles straining at that shirt. He can help with the loading and driving." There was no muscles evident.

"I'll stay and help Paw," William said. "We'll eversomuch miss our Jana, but it will be best for her."

"Then if it's decided, let's get started at daybust," Richard urged, lest the answer to his prayers shatter under examination. "I can't wait to get back *home* and see Anna."

CHAPTER TWENTY

Another Letter

Deana had never been sick. Therefore, when she cried the whole night through and refused to eat, Anna knew that the child was ill. Her body burned with fever. A frightened Anna hitched the horse to the small chaise she found in the barn and headed for Mesilla, glad for the calash top as a protection from sun and wind. She hoped there was a doctor in town.

The physician, an older man whose hair sprouted only on the extreme rear of his head, clucked his tongue in a scolding manner when he looked into Deana's throat. "Here's the culprit," he said. "An infected throat. And her ears likely ache, too."

"What . . . what caused it?" asked Anna.

"It's common to children," the doctor said. "Soot from the trains is bad for youngsters. Or the move to a different climate could have brought it on. It isn't serious yet, but it could get that way if not treated. You did well to bring her in with the first fever. A stitch in time saves nine."

"You'll have to *stitch* her throat?"

The doctor threw back his head and roared. "That's an old adage, my dear. No, there'll be no stitching. What she needs is a dose of my special compound and juices. The medicine is expensive, but it beats going to the pesthouse. We'll give her a dollop before you leave." He brought out the concoction and charged Anna seventy-five cents. "That should do it, but if not, bring her back and we'll try something else."

Before Anna reached the town's limits, a leather strap on the shay snapped, and she was obliged to have it repaired before she could go on home. The smithy outfitted the carriage with new leathers and replaced a cracked wheel. "It's been setting too long," he said, and billed her for two dollars.

She hadn't expected these hidden expenses, and they brought her to the brink of despair. Why had she thought that she, scarcely more than a child herself, could handle life's emergencies single-handedly?

What would she do? The thought of returning to Lubbock repulsed her. Corine had her own baby now, and there would be no room for extra family members in the one-room hut. Going back to Mary Butler was the lesser of two evils, but she couldn't even bear that solution. She had had a taste of her land and would never be satisfied anywhere else, living with someone else.

With a sickening panic, she faced a new thought. She had no money to go anywhere! She couldn't keep her land; she couldn't even pay her taxes! She felt defenseless, shorn of her stubborn confidence.

While she sat in the shade of a tree holding Deana and waiting for the carriage repair, Jake Nagel passed by. "Anna Lewis a'ready!" He pulled his horse to an abrupt halt.

"How is your mother?" asked Anna.

"She's in health a'ready. She's home stirrin' the sots in her bread to make it rise yet for dinner."

"And Leonianie and the rest of the children?"

"Fiddle fine."

"Please give them my regards."

"Regardless?"

"Tell them that I asked about them."

"I'll glad. And oh, yes. The letter man said if we saw you a'ready to day you have a mail at the post box."

"Thanks, Jake. I'll drop by for it."

"You dropped it?"

"I'll get it. I had planned to go by the post office and purchase a penny stamp anyhow. I need to write to a friend of mine."

Jake looked at the toes of his battered boots then up again with a close-guarded expression as if afraid his thoughts would show. "A man friend a'ready?"

"No. A dear lady named Mary with whom I . . . we lived for a while."

"Maw said till December a'ready when I'm seven-teened, I could sit with you Sundays if I didn't too late. She said I'd be old enough a'ready to take my own head in fer things—and that you was only a year past me a'ready. I'll wash my feet and wear a neckercher and my best bib and tucker and look a man's part." His mane of shaggy hair rioted around the back edge of his shirt collar. "I'm skimpy yet, but size don't make nuthin'. Maw said since you didn't black dress no more fer grieving, your past was over a'ready."

Anna's pain, having no outlet, could only tear and bruise her heart. The hurt wouldn't go away.

147

"I will grieve forever, Jake." She said it with a trace of irritation. "And I'll never 'sit' with anyone, on Sunday or any other day. For me, love had only one blossom—and the perfume from that blossom will sustain me for the rest of my life. I want no other . . . ever."

"But who will do the man things fer you a'ready, Missus Anna? Who will win your bread for you a'ready? I could bring milk and butter when I Sunday with you a'ready."

Anna smiled in an abstract, overcordial manner at this boy-man turned man-boy. "I don't know, Jake, but God and I will make it somehow."

"I'll wait a'ready," Jake said. "I got nobody'd be better'n you a'ready. You'll get a change in your head fer things yet when lonesome lets in." He slapped the reins across the steed's flanks and barreled off.

He had said she had a letter. Who would be writing to her? Who would know where she was? She decided it must be from the nice librarian in Lubbock who had taken her to the train station. She should have let the woman know that she arrived safely. But that would mean buying *two* penny stamps.

When she called for the letter and the man behind the iron-grated window handed it to her, she recognized the handwriting and swallowed a lump in her throat. It was from Jason.

"Another letter from Daddy," she told Deana, who had ceased her fretting, "but I can't read it yet any more than I could read the others. The hurt is still too raw. How this one letter got itself separated from the others, I don't know. And who sent it on here, I don't know either. We'll lay it up with the others . . . and someday when we're purged of our tears, we'll read them all and remember. . . ."

The west wind had taken a fragrance that made the fall air heady, but Anna scarcely took notice. After she bought milk for Deana and the few supplies that they needed, her finances were pitifully dwindled again. Eddies of fear crept up to the banks of her courage, and she felt the erosion beginning. It was a strange sensation knowing that there was no one on earth to turn to.

Once back inside her home, though, she made herself a cup of hot tea and added three teaspoons of sugar. Then she filled the tin bath, enjoying the embrace of warm water—and repeated her and Jason's verse of Scripture: *What time I am afraid, I will trust. . . .*

CHAPTER TWENTY-ONE

The Banker's Call

Anna took her pole and headed for the river. It teemed with fish, and she had developed her own recipe for fish chowder.

By some miracle, she had made it for a month. Reason told her she couldn't, but she did even though she felt a whole decade older than she had on the day the blade that cut her heart had fallen so swiftly. *But I can't hold out much longer*, she told herself. *I need coal oil for the lamps, more flour and milk.*

She tried to block out the future. Right now all she needed was a few nice fat grasshoppers for bait. . . .

The grasshoppers were fast, jumping away just as she clamped her hand down for the capture. The dry, cool air gave them energy. Chasing them farther and farther from the house, she found herself on a trickle of an overgrown path. Brambles and fallen branches grabbed at her petticoats.

Ensconced in a cul-de-sac of trees, worn and twisted by the years, she found an abandoned cabin. Could this be the dwelling once occupied by the Lewis family? The door stood partly ajar, and she pushed at it as if she would unwrap a precious package. Jason had lived here! A kaleidoscope of moods swept through her: a sadness at the cabin's disrepair, a joy that she had found it, and a desire to restore it to its better days.

Inside there was nothing to see but bare walls and bare floors chinked with mortar. But at least it *had* floors, a luxury that the Lewis family had not had since. It was sturdy yet and could be transformed into cozy living quarters. The thought of fixing it up brought a tingle of excitement. She found an old broom in the corner and swept the floor clean, clearing away the lacy cobwebs stretched face high. She would want to come back here often.

Outside and a few paces from the sagging front stoop, Anna found the grave of Corine's firstborn. She supposed that Richard had carved the hardwood cross that graced it. Or was it Jason? What must Corine have suffered? She'd had a bleak life by any reckoning. Like a cord stretched between her and her stepmother, Anna felt a sudden tug of sympathy. Corine was lonely, bitter and heartbroken, yet her nature wouldn't let her cry. Anna had been too young to understand a mother's grief. Corine had ruled by an iron hand disguised by no glove at all, but it was simply her defense against fear.

The memories made Anna pensive. She abandoned her plans to fish and turned back toward the house. They'd have porridge again today, and she'd fish tomorrow. She was caught in a riot of feeling.

A horse stood near her front door, and a well-dressed rider doffed his hat before she could shrink back into the sun-speckled shadows. Some third eye told her that this was the banker and that he had come to collect the taxes.

Her emotions surged at the expense of her stomach. She had hoped to stay on her land a few days longer. . . .

The man dismounted with a flourish and introduced himself as Mr. Fleming. His hair was the color of an old cello, disciplined by axle grease. It lay in handsome natural waves. His perpetual smile suggested that he found joy in the world and its inhabitants.

"Miss Elliott?" he greeted.

"Lewis," Anna corrected.

"Oh, yes, I recall the family who took you with them was named Lewis. I hope that you are enjoying your lovely Eden here and that there's not a serpent anywhere. I find that you are quite as lovely as your surroundings." His voice reminded her of warm rain. She spurned the flattery, afraid it was but a preamble to the dread proclamation.

"I'm sorry I missed you when you were in town," he said.

Anna said nothing.

"We need to talk a little business if we may. Shall we go inside, perhaps to your table?"

Anna went ahead of him and opened the door.

"Ah, the same table," mused Mr. Fleming, overriding Anna's silence. "I sat in this house many a time and had coffee with your father. It is wonderful to be back."

"Mr. Roper told me about . . . Father."

"I suppose you don't remember your parents at all?"

"Sometimes I imagine that I do. Then it's like . . . like a dream blinked away."

"You were quite young."

Anna's lips were unsteady, and her long fingers twined and untwined. "Mr. Roper said that you had seen after the

153

place and had paid the taxes for me all these years." To delay the crux with small talk was pointless.

"It certainly has been my pleasure."

"I'm afraid that I'll . . . I'll never be able to pay . . ."

Mr. Fleming spread a page of yellowed parchment on the table. "I'll read your father's will, if I may," he said. "In the Name of God, Amen. I bequeath to my children any houses and lands and estates. Share and share alike. Hereto I affix my hand and seal in the presence of witnesses." Reuben Elliott had signed the document with large, masculine strokes.

"And since I am the only survivor, I would be responsible for the . . . the taxes?"

"You are the recipient of all your father's properties and liabilities."

"I can't . . . pay the taxes . . . now. If I could have more time . . ."

"I took care of that for you. The taxes are not delinquent. You do plan to keep the place, don't you, Anna?" He cleared his throat. "I trust that I may call you Anna without offense."

"Oh, yes! I do plan to keep the place. Or, that is, I *want* to keep it. I will have to work out a plan, a way to manage here. But how will I ever—?"

"I don't see that you should have a problem."

"If . . . if I can find a way to earn a living."

"Please let me explain, Anna. I'm sure you can hire help with the farming. Your father had planned to invest in cattle and build a new barn as well as an improved tenant cabin. He had been in to talk with me about it. He had the money to do so. But the raid came before he had the chance. Therefore, he left a sizable sum of money in the

154

bank when he died.

"Your father's money has been multiplying itself all these years—growing like little green apples. Now the apples are yours for the picking. But take care. Sometimes a hungry child eats too many at once and gets a stomachache." He winked.

"After taxes, there is money left?"

"Oh, absolutely! Plenty of money. There's enough to last you for many years if you are a wise steward of what has been entrusted to you. And, of course, I am at your service, Anna. Will you take the Elliott name back as proprietor of your father's ranch, or will you keep the name of the family who reared you?"

Anna's cheeks pinked. "I'm a *real* Lewis now, Mr. Fleming. I married the Lewis's son, Jason."

"And is your husband here? He can help you—"

"He . . . he's gone. I . . . I lost him to death. I'm a widow."

"At such a young age? I'm sure you'll remarry someday. And I must give you a fatherly warning. Not all men are scrupulous. Some would seek your hand for your fortune. It could pose a problem."

"I have no plans of remarriage—ever."

"I take it that your loss has been quite recent. Time heals—"

"There are some things that time cannot heal, Mr. Fleming." She changed the subject. "I knew nothing of my family history until quite recently. I had never heard the Elliott name and didn't know about this land. Then I found my sister's diary—"

"Your sister?"

"Yes. She escaped from the Indians and was picked up

by a wagon train."

"Then it is my duty to locate her also."

"She's dead. She died en route from California to Oklahoma last year, and now I have her baby."

"The will makes no stipulations for grandchildren."

"I will give Deana her mother's part when she is of age."

"That is between you and your conscience."

"And in legal matters, I will trust to your advice if I may, Mr. Fleming."

"I had hoped that you would trust me as your father did."

"If I could be allotted so much a month for living expenses?"

"We won't cut you short, Anna. I'll be glad to help you with a budget. Can you and the baby live on fifty dollars a month?"

Fifty dollars! Whatever would she do with that much money each month? She was wealthy!

"And another thing. Some of the land in the northern part of our territory has the Midas touch in the form of black gold: oil. There has been no report of any in our area, but there's always the chance of an isolated find. Some of the gushers bring in as high as forty-six barrels a day. Shysters may be coming through testing the soil and trying to buy land. They might try to take advantage of a lone woman. Don't sign anything until you talk with me."

"This is my *home*, Mr. Fleming. One doesn't sell one's home for any amount of money."

After Mr. Fleming took his leave, Anna wanted to laugh, wanted to cry. If only she had someone with whom to share the good news! She had passed through a dark valley, and now she could find peace in the knowledge that she and Deana would make it.

No amount of money would ever take Jason's place. Any happiness she had would be an unsatisfactory sort of happiness in spite of her great thankfulness for a means of survival.

Anna crawled into bed that night and hugged herself like a child with no one to comfort her. *Jason, if I could have had all this and you, too, life would have been perfect!*

Some days would be pleasant, some desperately lonely. The pain of losing Jason would throb forever, but the future of her land no longer tolled mortality.

She braided her hair, blew out the lamp, and cried herself to sleep.

CHAPTER TWENTY-TWO

No Answer

Jason rode hard toward the house with the sleeping Jana against his shoulder.

Anna. A halo of golden hair . . . sapphire blue eyes filled with girlish innocence. Anna, his bride, his wife. . . . The thought of her had never tasted so sweet.

She would have gotten his letter by now, and she would be expecting him. Any sadness, any evil, any trouble in the world would become inconsequential when they were together again. Life would be complete—bright and young and new in their own home.

The last drops of sunlight melded with dusk as he left Mesilla, but he couldn't wait for morning. What if—? No, he couldn't let his mind become a campground for the thought that she might not be there.

Between rags of cloud, a brilliant moon splashed light, shadowing the side of the house. His horse whinnied, bringing a responsive call from Caballocita.

He dismounted and ran to the door, almost stumbling over a raccoon that dipped his food in the water that Anna had set out. "Anna!" he called.

There was no answer.

"Anna! Open the door!" He knocked loudly.

When he still roused no one, he went to the bedroom window and pressed his nose against the glass like a child peering into a clear cookie jar. He couldn't see beyond the gauzy curtains. "Let me in, dear!" He pecked on the pane with his knuckles.

A voice, more like a high, shaky croak, pleaded from within, "Go away! Please go away!"

Then Anna didn't live here! His heart, rent with anguish and loss, protested against the unendurable. He'd made the trip in vain.

Where was Anna? Hope drained away, and his mind filled with questions and uncertainties. It was overpowering.

On his way back to his horse, he kicked over a tub turned upside down, bringing a terrible volume of noise to the deep, fronded silence of the night. The raccoon skittered away.

Jason's mind gnawed away at his problems. Where would he and Jana spend the night? If he went back into town, he wouldn't know where to find lodging there. He dare not sleep on the ground with a child so small.

Would the householders mind if he took shelter in the small cottage that was once his home? He could pay them in the morning. He couldn't blame them for not getting up to admit a stranger into their home in the middle of the night. This country had a history of bandits and outlaws. He would apologize for the disturbance tonight and explain that he thought his wife lived in the house. The residents would surely understand—and forgive. If it were not for Jana, he could sleep anywhere, but she must be protected from the elements, from wild animals, and from the world at large. If anything happened to Jana, Richard and Corine—

and especially William—could not bear the loss.

He urged the horse along the ribbon of a trail that led to the cabin. The closer he got to the cottage, the more familiar the surroundings. Silver-gray moonlight washed the scene. The trees he had climbed were still there, like aged soldiers. Some had lost limbs, but they were still valiant. Had it really been sixteen years since he had been along this path?

He tied the animal and went into the cabin. He was not ready for the rush of emotions that came surging back. The days spent here were the "good days": the picking of wild berries when you couldn't stop because there was always one more place to try; floor-sweep on the wooden floor, crumbly underfoot; the farm wagon with its rough bench; his mother's laughter and singing, curiously remote.

The cabin seemed filled with the essence of another human being—warm—as if someone had just left. It had been cleaned recently, and a smell of lavender tormented his senses. He reached for some memory that was just beyond him, and as he reached for it, it edged away and vanished into the shadows.

A mattress lay in one corner of the room with a baby quilt spread out on it. This wouldn't have been something that his mother left, and if she had, it would be riddled by time now. And there was a rocking chair. Had he invaded someone's private domain? No one was about the place.

Whoever had taken over the property had foiled his plans. This is where he had hoped to house his father and mother. They would soon be on their way, and when they arrived, he would have no provisions for them.

They had been excited about returning to a familiar place, a place that echoed happiness. Tomorrow, he would have to go back into town and post them a letter telling them not to come here. He hoped he might stop them before they departed.

Now what would he do with Jana? He would be obliged to return her to his parents and begin his search for Anna. She was probably still in Lubbock. He had followed someone else's word that she had traveled to New Mexico.

The mental battle raged again, gathering ammunition. Why didn't she leave him word that she was moving to another lodging? She knew that he would look for her at the hotel, expecting her to be there. Did the man at the hotel purposely throw him off?

And why hadn't Anna answered any of his letters? That was the greatest mystery of all. He'd asked her to write and let him know if she needed more money. He'd encouraged her to remain where she was until he came for her. He'd even told her that if there were insurmountable problems, she could get back on the train and return to Byers Bend. And he'd never heard one word from her!

How would his parents survive the winter on the Texas plains? His father's sweat had seeped into the soil, leaving him as dry and parched as old leather. They'd given everything, stinting themselves, spurning luxuries. There was nothing more to give—and certainly nothing to receive.

Jason lay the child down on the mattress, but his own thoughts were on the edge of a precipice. He must stay awake and make a plan and fill out the details of that plan. . . . He couldn't give in to hopeless confusion!

Just as the first pinstripe of muted daylight slanted through the window, Jason lost his battle and slept the long, loglike sleep of a spent man.

CHAPTER TWENTY-THREE

Reunion

Lances of sunlight pierced the autumn dawn. Anna yawned, shrugging off a sleepless night. By day, the terrors of the darkness seemed less intimidating. However, a couple of events remained in her mind along with the general hysteria of the midnight hours.

She was sure that she had heard someone call her name. She had jerked sharply upright, shaking. She thought it was a man's voice, but the sound was drowned by the thud of her heart.

Then she remembered that a shadow blocked out the moonlight in the window. She could attach no identity to the shadow except a dim grayness—and after a moment it had faded into blackness. Her throat constricted, and in half-swallowed words she called out for the apparition to go away. And it did.

She imagined hearing a horse leave, but as the night wore on and her composure crept back, she decided that her mind, receptive soil for the seeds of fear, had created a monster of torment from the dust of her dreams. No one would have a reason to roam about such an isolated place.

Something had disturbed her, though, and she was still awake, trying to figure out what it could have been. Her friendly raccoon! That was it! But raccoons didn't talk, and she remembered her name being called. . . . Or did she? It was likely a dream—a very realistic dream.

An eagerness for the new day, too complex to unravel and springing from some untapped source, brought her out of bed. She chose her most colorful dress. Her hair would be allowed to fend for itself until time to go into town for her draw at the bank to buy supplies.

Today it seemed that some new resource gathered cautiously within her, healing but still tender. This might even be the day that she would open all of Jason's letters and read them. Her spirit and mind blended in a tangled harmony. Something had soothed her troubled soul, though it was a nameless sensation from a nameless source.

She caught sight of herself in the chiffonier mirror. The dark shades of fatigue under her eyes only made them the more noticeable.

She had one more item to take to the cabin on which she had been working as a "playhouse" for herself and Deana. It was a bucket with a dipper. There was a well behind the building, and when they had their picnics there, they would have water. Deana especially enjoyed the outings and the little house.

Nothing seemed amiss when Anna took Deana to the cabin that morning. The leaves looked like rainbows, one color blending into another, unbearably beautiful. It was a smiling day. Jason's horse, tied on the opposite side of the house from her approach, made no move.

She pushed open the door and burst in, babbling to Deana about their "fun place" in the woods—and stopped in her tracks. On the pallet she had laid for herself and Deana was a man and a baby! She let out a small cry of surprise and dropped the bucket and its dipper with a clatter. She started to back away hurriedly.

The commotion awoke Jason, and he turned his face toward her. "*Anna!*" His hair and clothes were rumpled from sleep. "My darling Anna!" His feet tangled in the coverlet when he tried to get up.

She gave a wild, sweet scream and sank into the chair. Was this the stuff of her fevered imagination? She couldn't believe it; her mind mocked hope. "But Jason, I thought you were dead! Willy said—"

Jason was beside her, wrenching her up like a drowning victim toward air, then kissing the dark hollows that smudged under her eyes. "I wrote you that I was coming, darling. Didn't you get my letter?"

"Yes, I . . . I did, but I didn't read it."

"You didn't read it? But why?"

"I thought . . . I thought . . . Oh, let's talk about what I thought and the whys later!" She sat Deana on the floor and buried her face in his chest, clinging to him as if he might escape in midair. "Just now, I . . . I want to make sure I'm not dreaming! Oh, *Jason!*"

"I came to the house last night and called and called—"

"Was that you? Can you forgive me, my sweetheart? I was so scared . . . I didn't know . . ."

The lines at the corners of his eyes spoke his overflowing happiness. "It is enough that I have found you, my lovely Anna!"

Each look at Jason seemed to revive Anna. *This is like waking from a nightmare*, she thought. *It is life I have awakened to. Life and love and happiness.* The breeze sang morning, the birds sang resurrection. Triumphantly it blazed. *Hurry, while it lasts!*

Jana sat up, bright-eyed and startled.

"And where did you get that beautiful baby, Jason?"

"This is my baby sister. I went by and found Maw and Paw starving to death, Anna. Maw looks pitiful. They were eating prickly pear jelly. I asked God what we could do to help them, and I feel we should bring them here if you don't mind."

"Mind? Why, I'd love it, Jason! Your thoughtfulness as a son is only exceeded by your chivalry as a husband!"

"You have a way of making a man feel ten feet tall, Anna."

"And they let you bring this delightful child on ahead?"

"Yes. They can travel faster without her, and Maw wasn't feeling well. I came by train. They're all so crazy about this baby, they would die if anything happened to her on the trip. Especially Willy. He made her a wooden doll and sent it along. He sent one for Deana, too."

"The famous dilly-dolly!" Anna's laughter boomed up. "He told me about the dolls he planned to make from the millinery spools. Willy is clever."

"Jana and her dilly-dolly are inseparable."

"Jana! Is that her name?"

"They named her for us—you and me. Jana is for Jason and Anna."

"I'm flattered. How . . . how did they accept our marriage, Jason?"

"Maw half expected it all along. Paw was pleased when he got used to the idea. And Willy was absolutely ecstatic. Maw was contrite for her treatment of you and sends her amends."

"I hold no ill feelings, Jason. Through my own suffering, I have become more compassionate. Your mother suffered more than her share. We will try to make their last years the very best of their lives. We'll build them a bigger and better house than this one—a house that looks out over the river."

"Yes, in time. But they're coming right away, and it will take . . . money. We must start making money before we can spend it!"

"We have plenty."

"Plenty?"

"My father left us well fixed, Jason. From now to the New Jerusalem."

"Did you know . . . before you came?"

"No, I had a few frightening days before the banker came to explain my inheritance. I even learned to fish! I can make larruping fish chowder!"

"I am distressed that you suffered deprivation, my dear."

"We experienced no permanent damage."

"Are we having fish chowder today? It sounds good to me."

"I was going in today for our allotment, and to pick up some veal."

"We'll go together."

"We'll go everywhere together from now on, Jason Lewis. I won't let you out of my sight. Besides, I want to show you off to Jake Nagel and Mr. Fleming and Mr. Roper and—"

"Whoa! Have *all* these been pursuing the gorgeous young widow?" Jason teased.

"The widow told each of them that her heart belonged

to one and one only—dead or alive—for all eternity!"

"Let's take our babies and go home," Jason suggested. "I'm anxious to start *living*."

CHAPTER TWENTY-FOUR

Full Cup

"Maw and Paw won't mind living in the tiny cabin until we can get another built," Jason said. "Willy can stay with us if it's too crowded."

"When do you think they will arrive?"

"Any day now. Paw said he'd make good time."

"You left them enough money for the trip?"

"I did. And if they sell their property for cash, that will give them even more."

The day of Anna and Jason's conversation, however, was the day they got the letter in their "tree-holler" mailbox. It was from William.

"Read it quickly, Jason!" Anna clapped her hands like an eager child whose sudden impulses—which might or might not be logical—needed instant gratification. "Surely it will tell us when they are coming!"

Dear Jason and Anna, he read. *This letter sends good greetings to your family and to my sweet Jana. But with worse tidings. The day before our start to New Mexico, Paw stepped in a prairie dog hole and broke his leg just above the ankle. He was so pained*

169

in it that I took him to the doctor. (The same doctor that gave Maw the tonic.) The doctor said it was a bad turn and he splinted Paw's ankle and said Paw couldn't do no traveling until six months was over. Since the place was sold already, I prayed to God to know what to do. The man who bought it wouldn't sell it back to us for what he gave for it and he had no mercy. He only allowed us a week to get moved out.

I asked myself what would Jason do if he was here and what would he say if I could talk to him. It took most of the money you left to pay the doctor bill. Paw said we must save the money we got out of the place for the trip and to get ourselves settled. So I went to town and offered myself for work at the blacksmith shop. Josh's paw said if I could work real hard from sunup to sundown, he would pay me a man's wage. This is the happy part. Josh's paw knew where there was a house for rent. If I took it for the whole six months and paid the whole of it at the start, I could have it for four dollars a month the owner said. It is a palace of a place with a clay tile floor and water piped in and a bathtub inside for Maw and Paw. It has an icebox that takes a ten-pound block of ice and a good cookstove with four lids and a warming shelf. (I set Paw's slippers on the warming shelf and get them warm to help his hurting.)

Paw pitched a fit about the high price of the rent, but I will be making fifty cents a day. I will have eight dollars a month left over for food and Maw's medicine and that should do us grand until we leave. We all miss Jana fretfully. I cry secret for her some nights and I know that Maw and Paw do, too, but there's no *need to try to bring her back to us now. With my job-bing I couldn't help Maw care for her and she isn't able to care for a baby all by herself. And Paw can't get around.*

I got the tombstone moved off the grave that wasn't yours, Jason. If I knew who the fellow was who got him-self killed, I'd change the name because it's a sad pity not to be tagged when you're dead.

Maw and Paw talk about when they get back to their home in New Mexico every day. Paw says it will be more like heaven than anywhere else. He grieves that he ever left. Babies forget fast, so don't let Jana forget me. Tell her it was Willy that made her the dilly-dolly. Tell her every day.

This is a long letter and I'm not good at knowing where to break off into paragraphs. I decided I had rather you be straining your eyes reading than straining them looking down the road for Paw's wagon for the next six months. Affection, William E. Lewis.

Jason folded the letter reverently. "I'm proud of Willy," he said. "He has the makings of a man."

"His ambition is to be like you."

"Strange," Jason chuckled. "My ambition is to be like him."

"This will give us more time to get everything ready for them," Anna said in an effort to lift Jason's spirits. She could see that the letter had affected him. "We could have their new house built by then!"

"I'm thinking we should wait and let them pick their own location for the house," Jason said. "Maw might be ill at ease with a house on the river because of the baby.

With so many losses, she tends to be overprotective—"

"You're right, of course, Jason. And they might have their own wishes and ideas about the floor plan. We should wait and let them have a say."

"Willy made a valid point in his letter. It is important that we keep the memory of her family alive in Jana's mind. When we give her the dilly-dolly, we'll say 'Willy made it' every time."

"I know they miss her dreadfully."

"You don't mind keeping her longer, do you, dear?"

"Oh, no! She's a joy. She's a dear, sweet child. I think she has your nature. When we took the girls to town last Saturday, a lady asked me if they were twins! One with fair skin and golden hair and the other with olive skin and black hair!"

"But you had them dressed alike."

"Yes, in the dresses that Mary Butler made. Oh, Jason! I must write to the Butlers. I wrote them that you had been killed. And I got so excited with your coming that I didn't let them know that you are alive."

"Write them today, Anna. Mary will grieve herself ill. She clucked over me like a mother hen. And now when she should be the happiest—with the children."

"The children?"

"I wrote you about the children."

"Remember, I didn't read the letters. I thought you were dead, and I couldn't bear to look at them—"

"They put in for two children from the orphan train: a boy and a girl. They were waiting for them most impatiently when I left."

"What is an orphan train?"

"The Children's Aid Society in New York put out an

appeal for couples in rural America to take immigrants and orphans and crowded city children. Mary said they were called 'streets' because they slept in doorways and cartons and got their food by stealing or selling their bodies."

"In our America, Jason?"

"In our America. There was no age stipulation, and Mary said they'd be better off with an old maw and paw than none at all."

"Mayhap we could take some of those children, Jason."

"Dear Anna! You have your hands full! I don't have but one selfish bone in my body. More children would mean less time for me!"

She gave a little leap and landed in his arms. "There'll always be time for you, Jason Lewis!"

"And please write to Maw and Paw, too, Anna."

"Why don't we send them a little money each month?"

"My generous queen! God will bless you for your thoughtfulness."

"If He gives me any *more* blessings, I'll *die* of an overdose of happiness! I have you and Deana and Jana— and we'll soon have your family, too!"

Her cup, she decided, was indeed running over.

CHAPTER TWENTY-FIVE

The Discovery

The months fell away as if Anna and Jason had never been apart.

In the spring, Jason put in the crops and planted a vegetable garden large enough for both Anna and his maw. Around the small cottage where his folks would live temporarily, he planted flowers. He remembered that Corine had flowers when she lived there before. Multicolored zinnias. Marigolds. Cockscomb. Pansies.

Richard's progress was chronicled by Willy. His leg was healing on schedule. They were managing well but eager to see Jana again.

Anna's time was swallowed up with her two toddlers. She called them her "Lewis and Clark Expedition." "They want to explore everything," she laughed. "I'm as busy as a maw with quintuplets. I need six pairs of hands!"

"What you need is a little walk out-of-doors," Jason said, lifting her chin and brushing back a lock of rebellious hair. "There's nothing like a walk in the woods to put life in its proper perspective and give one strength. I want to show you the wispy ferns, like old feather dusters, and the toadstools that remind me of yellow cushions—"

"Lead the way!"

Jason picked up one girl and Anna the other, and they tramped across several acres of their land—land begemmed with soft hues of the season's early blooms. After a while, they broke out into a clearing where the land flattened out and the trees became scarce.

"Let's rest a minute," Jason said.

"Yes, let's."

"Have you ever noticed that nature's colors never clash?"

"Now that you mention it—" She broke off. "What have you found now, Jason? A new kind of plant?"

Jason looked down at his feet and then stooped to examine the earth. "No. It's a . . . sinkhole. Watch where you step, dear."

The depression in the earth oozed with a shiny black liquid. Jason dipped his finger in it and sniffed.

"What does it smell like?"

He wrinkled his nose. "Tar."

"What is it?"

He tried to bridle his excitement. "I think, Anna, that this is what the whole world is going crazy over: black gold. It appears that we may have a vein of oil on our land."

"Oil? Jason! Mr. Fleming said that oil is selling for a dollar a barrel! It is being used for fuel, he said. The government wants it. Farther north, a company named Keystone is leasing land and drilling. But Mr. Fleming said there was no oil in this area—"

"Sometimes there's an underground pool that is isolated from other minerals."

"We could contact that Keystone company."

"I don't want to lease our land, Anna. I want to drill for the oil myself. It will be expensive to buy the equipment, but it will pay off in the long run. If you can trust me . . ."

"I do trust you! What will we need?"

"A little steam engine."

"Buy it, Jason. Buy anything you need."

They returned to the house and spent the evening discussing the discovery. "There may not be enough oil to cover the cost of drilling, Anna. We're not in the oil basin's perimeter. Our little bit may not be worth the effort to bring up. If we fail, we will have squandered a lot of money."

"We won't fail, Jason. I feel it here." She laid her hand over her heart. "God put the oil there—on our land only."

Jason wasted no time. With Mr. Fleming egging him on, he made a trip to El Paso and found an engine. The next week, he began drilling. At first, only muddy water bubbled up, and Jason fought a spasm of disappointment. Then came a rushing sound. Black liquid squirted up. They had a gusher!

He turned off the engine and made a mad dash for the house. "Anna! Anna!"

"What has happened, Jason? Are you hurt?"

"We have a gusher! Get the horsecar and go into town! Tell Mr. Fleming to send buyers with barrels while I dig a slush pit to keep the oil from drowning us!"

The twenty-four-barrel-a-day gusher kept Jason on the run for several days. "And to think, Anna, that our well brings in twice as much money in one *day* as Willy makes in a month!" Jason pointed out.

When the well blew itself out, Anna felt something akin to relief. "Now we can have a meal together again," she teased. "I've missed you."

Another letter came from Lubbock with unfavorable news. "We were obliged to get the doctor out for Maw," the message said. "He thinks she may have consumption. There is no cure. It is a God-bless that you have little Jana. Maw is not able to care for her. Paw is still crippling and has pain in the joint. I do the cooking and the cleaning when I get off work. We got a chance to buy the house here and not knowing for sure how long we would need it, Paw couldn't bear paying rent any longer. He said it was like pouring water on the ground. We'll come when everybody gets better."

Drilling the well put Jason behind on the crops. "Looks like Paw and Willy will have to build the new cottage themselves," he said. "I won't have time with the crops and all."

"Or we can hire it built," suggested Anna.

The year ended, and another started with its fast-paced cycle. Anna helped keep books, made many trips to the bank for Jason, and made clothes for all of them on her mother's treadle machine.

They found a small country church on the outskirts of Mesilla and went there to worship each Lord's Day. It was Anna's favorite day of the week, a day filled with sweet satisfaction. She liked dressing the girls in their starched frocks and bonnets, smelling their soap-scented skin. She enjoyed giving generously in the collection.

She was fond of the parson, a worn and aging man— worn from being directly in the path of sins and failures for so many years. And she liked his wife, whose face was finely cracked like the finish on an old vase. They were gentle country people who cared for their flock.

By the end of the second year, both girls were talking. When Jana hugged her dilly-dolly, she said, "Willy make it!" To which Deana, not to be outdone, would respond, "Willy make mine, too!"

Then the letter arrived saying that Richard Lewis had taken blood poisoning in his foot and died in his sleep. Corine was now too ill to make a move.

Jason made preparations to put everything aside and go to Lubbock. But before he could book passage, another letter came. Corine had followed her husband in death by just a few days. Willy, now nearing fifteen, had seen to it that they had "a proper Christian burial." He said he made them each "a nice box to sleep in." And he was making them a headstone.

"As soon as I can sell the house," he wrote, "I will catch the train to New Mexico and help with the raising of my baby sister. She is partly my responsibility, too. I can hardly wait to see her again! She will fill a crying spot in my heart and I cannot be complete without her." Evenings, he said, were his most difficult time, but they were better now, though still bad enough. Maw had found Jesus before she died, and to know that his parents were no longer suffering was his comfort.

Jason grieved over the passing of his parents—and Anna grieved along with him. "We don't have to sorrow like those who have no hope," she said. "I found it in the Bible."

"But I . . . I had such lovely plans for them!" he bemoaned.

"But God had lovelier plans, my sweetheart. No matter the earthly paradise we could have provided for them, it couldn't compete with God's paradise. We couldn't provide for them a pain-free life—so God did it for us."

"It must be so hard for William. We must pray that he will be here and be reunited with Jana—soon."

CHAPTER TWENTY-SIX

Lesley

Lesley Horn was ill-suited for the rigors of the range and coyote music—and hard work. He wore idleness like a comfortable shirt. Unskilled at farming, he hated it. There were no butlers or maids at his beck and call. He longed for a nice, unearned income.

When he heard at the tavern that oil flowed like water in New Mexico, his pitchfork eyes took on a calculating glaze. He had a deep envy for the trappings of wealth. Ah, yes! That first wife of his was heir to some land in that area. She had had some kind of moth-eaten papers that she guarded carefully. She kept them in the trunk. If he could just find them . . .

He heaved himself to his feet, long since past the milestone of steadiness.

"Where' ya goin', Horn?" asked a tipsy buddy.

"To get rich," he answered.

"That's a fat meat dream, Horn."

"I always get what I go after."

He lashed at his horse, filling the clean air with curses. He had to find that land deed! Underneath that land would be a bowl of oil, and he'd have his desserts. Then farewell it would be to this cow-infested prairie with its murderous weeds! It would take years to make one's fortune here. His father could have it all! He gave a wicked wink to an imaginary accomplice.

For some time now, Lesley had regretted his ill-considered gallop to the preacher and his marriage to the honey-tongued Bootsie. Her love had grown lukewarm before the marriage license was filed at the courthouse. She didn't cotton to print dresses and cornfields, and said as much. In the saloons, she was in her element. There she monopolized the limelight and loved it. On the range, she was a miserable wretch. She would be glad to give Lesley his freedom. But when he sported his diamonds and lived in a grand rancho with servants, she would gnash her teeth. Ah, sweet vengeance!

There might be something good come of that first mother-arranged marriage to the Elliott girl yet. He had quickly tired of her flour-pale face and lusterless eyes. She refused to paint! She hadn't wanted him to drink or gamble, either, and tried to send him on guilt trips. She was too religious, too goody-goody, to please his fancy. On several occasions he had struck her harshly for her stubborn piety. Yet all that he endured prior to her death would be worth it if he could get his hands on her oil-rich property in New Mexico. He would be sitting pretty!

He fell from his mount and tripped over the threshhold of his father's thrown-together shanty. The trunk! He lunged for it as a thirsty man for a bottle. In a frenzy, he threw the items that had belonged to his mother across the room trying to get to the bottom. He found a hidden bag of money and slipped it under his coat, but when he had removed every article, he found that there were no documents.

Black intensity smoldered in his eyes. What had become of those papers? He shook his head to clear his thoughts. Someone had stolen them! Malice burned in his spirit like a slow, hot underground fire.

That girl that his mother had picked to be his second wife! What was her name? Anna Lewis, that was it! She had been in the wagon when they crossed the river and staked their claim. She must have taken the land deed out of the trunk!

His memory grappled at something else. The baby! He had almost forgotten about her. That baby would qualify as a legal heir in the place of her deceased mother. The Anna woman knew that; that's why she was willing to take the baby on her honeymoon with her. The land belonged to the baby, and the baby belonged to *him*. He hadn't signed any adoption papers.

He'd get the property one way or another, with or without the deed. He was glad that he thought of the child. That would give him leverage. If he threatened to take the child, Anna might hand over the papers without a fuss. Women were funny about children once they got attached to them.

Anger came in fresh waves every few minutes. She thought she would get by with the theft, but he would show her. Wherever she was, she would pay for her crime. She might even be in New Mexico trying to take over the land and get the oil for herself. The thought made him half crazed.

Wait! Hadn't she married that Lewis boy named Jason? Lesley had been drinking the night she married, and his memory had gaps. Was that the same night he married Bootsie?

Perhaps the logical thing to do would be to go to the Lewises' adobe home out on the desert where he and his family had spent the night during a sandstorm. The Lewis family should know Anna's whereabouts.

He turned around to see his father, Philip Horn, watching him. Philip was a man with a bulk long past hope of disciplining into any shape. He filled the entire doorway. "What are you looking for, Lesley?"

"Those deeds to the New Mexico land."

"We lost them somewhere between California and here. They were worthless anyhow."

"You're as wrong as sin on Sunday, Popsie. Those papers are my ticket to easy street, and I plan to find them wherever they are. I'll be gone awhile, so you'll have to handle the *prosperity* here. Handsome farms . . . Shimmering yellow grain . . . *Anything* will grow . . . Your sweet milk clabbered, Popsie. I'm leaving." His eyes were like metal, and his words carried a curt finality.

"Where is my money bag, Lesley?"

"What money bag?"

"You can't take my money, Lesley!"

Lesley's cold eyes were veiled with hostility. "You remind me of Solomon in the Bible, Popsie. He stayed all wrought up, afraid his sons would spend his money after he'd checked out. I'll just take the money now so you don't have to worry about what will become of it later. It will save me a gambling game and get me to my destination faster."

"Please, son! That is my life's savings!"

"It doesn't become you to be a beggar."

"Lesley!" Philip's voice broke. "You good-for-nothing—!"

"Goodbye, Popsie. I haven't the time for the usual exchange of insults. I'm going out to seek my fortune like a good little pig. You can stay here and get filthy while I go and get *filthy rich*. Ha. Ha." He stumbled over the same threshhold as he left.

In Purcell, Lesley bought a ticket to Lubbock and slept off a hangover for most of the trip. Once in Lubbock, his craving for liquor got the best of him and landed him in the bar. Before he became too soused to remember, he asked at the counter if anyone knew a farmer named Lewis.

"There's a Willy Lewis workin' at th' smithy," volunteered a local drunk. "His paw up and died, and his maw is graveyard bound if she ain't there already."

Lesley recognized Willy's name. "Did they use to live 'way out on the desert?"

"Yessiree. Towards La Mesa. Sold to a land grabber."

"Where could I find this Willy boy?"

"At the smithy, I told ye."

The next day, Leslie found Willy, but Willy was unwilling to talk. However, Lesley knew how to put on a saintly front. He'd had years of practice.

"Anna is keeping my little girl," he said, "and she said that I could visit with her anytime my daddy-heart got lonesome. I don't aim to bother Anna or the child. I just want to satisfy my mind that she is well—and I have a little money to give her. Them bitsy ones can wrap a body around their finger."

"Yes, they can," sighed William. "I have a wee sister myself."

"Then you know—"

"Anna married my brother, Jason," Willy said.

"Yes, I know that. I gave her my blessings. The blame lies on me for her sudden change of plans. We were betrothed—Anna and I—but I let her down." He let contrition drip from his voice. "You see, I married another woman, and that hurt Anna. That left her with no home, no husband, and no family up in Oklahoma. My own mother died, and Anna felt abandoned. Your brother came along at the opportune time, and I implored him to wed Anna. But by then, Anna had attached herself to my baby, so I gave her my permission to keep the child. Now I'm yearning for just a short visit . . . it has been so long." Lesley actually wiped away tears.

"They moved to New Mexico. As soon as I get this place sold, I'm going there, too."

Lesley had found out what he wanted to know. He made more small talk, then dismissed himself.

That day, he bought a ticket to El Paso.

CHAPTER TWENTY-SEVEN

Unwelcome Visitor

"**M**y steam engine played out, Anna, and I want to try some more drilling. I'll have to go to El Paso to have it repaired."

"Please get me some pretty cloth while you are there, Jason. The store at Mesilla has such a poor selection."

"I'll be glad to do that for you, my love. Is there anything else you need?"

"Only for you to hurry back."

"I'll have to be gone overnight."

"I understand, dear. Remember that I lived here alone for more than a month before you found me. I'm not frightened. I've never felt safer anywhere."

"I'll miss you."

"I hope that you do!"

"Take care of my girls."

Anna couldn't diagnose her feeling when Jason left that morning. It was akin to a sense of danger, but she scoffed at the sensation that refused to go away, scratching at her mind like a burr.

When Jason had gone, she couldn't sit still. She found

187

it hard to concentrate. Reading was impossible, as well as stitching. Her mind was like an untidy quilt box, full of scraps and raveled ribbons.

She tried to put her mind to Willy's arrival. Of course, there would be no call to build a house now. Willy would live with them. He would be a blessing to her overworked husband, but they must take care that Willy would have some leisure time to enjoy Jana, too. How he must have missed her! She had grown so much and was surprisingly intelligent for her three years.

At noon, with the sun resting like a traveler at the top of a mountain, she fed the girls and ate a few bites herself. Her stomach felt too uneasy for much; she was still restless. Deana was fussy and sleepy, but Jana, who had slept later that morning, still wanted to play. Anna put Deana down for a nap.

A gust of fresh air blew in at the front door, and Anna had the unpleasant feeling that someone had entered her house. Her scalp prickled.

She heard the soft outcry of a floorboard that said a foot was pressing it. Then came the crash of heavy boots, and Leslie, his face stone hard, stepped in front of her with the swiftness of a striking snake. Light from the kitchen window threw his face into a deep shadow—a shadow not quite deep enough to hide the hostile gleam in his eyes.

"I found you, Anna Lewis." There was no humor in his smile. "Here you sit with your fat purse and your life of luxury. You stole the land deeds that belonged to my deceased wife. This house, this land, all the oil rights belong to her—not to *you*. Therefore, it is mine and I *will have it!* You have no part nor lot in this matter, *Mrs.*

Lewis. I demand that land deed!"

His face wavered before her in a way that made her sick. She strained to keep the mounting anxiety out of her voice. She had to say the right thing to Lesley. She had faced his depraved nature before.

"I have stolen nothing, Lesley." She said it calmly, evenly, licking her dry lips with a tongue that trembled. "I was your first wife's sister. I was an Elliott, too, born right here in this house. My father left a will that gave me the land on which I live."

The revelation seemed to short-circuit Lesley's patience. "My daughter has rights, too! She has the rights of her mother, and since she is a minor, her rights are *my* rights. I *will* have the land, Anna, even if I have to kill someone to get it." It was an awful threat, made more awful by the violence with which it was said.

Anna reached into that special corner of her mind where she stored potential courage and found it empty. "I think we can be reasonable," she said. A haunting fear slowly fermented into torture and dried her mouth, leaving her with a strange tendency to swallow.

"I've no trace of a halo, as you well know, Anna. People who get in the way of the sickle get cut down." His eyes were weighty with purpose.

Oh, Jason, the source of my strength and my moral support, I need you!

"You are Deana's father," Anna said, her fear now a walking paralysis, "and Jason and I will see that Deana has her part of the inheritance. We will be fair with her when she is of age. I told the banker this."

"W*hen she is of age!*" he taunted. "And how many years of plenty will that cheat me out of? I'm like the lilies

189

of the field. I neither toil nor spin. It's time for *me* to have the plushy life awhile."

"Jason will be back soon and we can discuss this." A pain like a stab of a cold knife shot through her heart. She beat down the surge of hysteria that came with it.

"Your husband took the train out south this morning. I watched him go. He won't be back for a while. You and I will settle this ourselves." His eyes roamed idly around the room, and for the first time he seemed to notice Jana playing quietly in the floor with her doll.

Anna's mind froze into a solid block of panic, threatening to still even her breath. She held herself together, swallowing her tears while her body shook with crawling vibrations. She couldn't let him know how frightened she was. It would only incite his evil mind! *What time I am afraid, I will trust. . . .*

"What do you want, Lesley?"

"I want *everything*: the house, the land—and I may decide that I want you, too."

The burning of Anna's face spread to her neck and ears. *Oh, God*, she flung the silent prayer skyward, *send your angels to help me now!*

"You have a father's right to your child, but you have no right to me. I am a married woman."

"I'll have my child—until you produce the land deed . . ."

"The land deed isn't here. It is in the safety deposit box at the bank in town."

"You will sign everything over to me. Until then you will not see my child again." With those words, he swept Jana into his arms and headed for the door with long strides.

"No, Lesley! *No!* That's the wrong child! That isn't

your child!" Anna thought that she might faint. She pushed back the clammy darkness with a determined will.

He gave a snort of cruel laughter. "You're not the Sunday school girl you used to be, huh? First you stole my dead wife's papers, and now you lie to me."

"I'm not lying!"

"If you cause any trouble or put the law on my trail, I'll dispose of this child in a way that will chill your blood."

"Please, Lesley! Believe me. That's not—"

He was gone, taking Jana with him.

CHAPTER TWENTY-EIGHT

Threats

The sick thudding of Anna's heart built remorselessly until it seemed to explode, sending shrapnel of anguish up, down, and around her body. Her mind felt sluggish and cold, congealing the dread that iced in her breast. Dreadful prospects ate away at her spirit like soul termites.

What would Lesley Horn do to the innocent child? Where would he take her? Thinking her his own, he might exercise a sadistic pleasure in his ownership. Gentleness—or even rational thinking—was not in the warp and woof of his fiber. He was a dangerous man.

Jana's dilly-dolly lay sprawled on the floor, bringing another fiery prong of pain to Anna's head. She picked it up, hugged it, and cried herself dry of tears.

When Deana awoke, she joined in the sorrow, asking for Jana "to play wiff me." She ran from room to room searching for her playmate.

Anna wept the night through, and Jason found her sobbing when he returned home. "My Anna! My Anna!" he soothed. "Whatever has happened? Are my girls all right?"

"No, Jason. It's Jana—" She buried her face in her hands.

"What is it, Anna? Where is she? Is she . . . hurt badly?"

"I don't know. Lesley Horn came and took her away."

"Lesley Horn?"

"Ye–yes."

"Then that was Lesley Horn who followed me in town yesterday."

"He said he saw you."

"He pulled his hat over his face so that I wouldn't recognize him. The yellow coward! And he came here?"

"It was . . . frightening. I thought I would . . . faint."

"I can't dwell on the thought, darling. It makes me have . . . unholy feelings inside. It makes me want to get even—and God said, 'Vengeance is mine; I will repay.' But why did he take Jana instead of his own child?"

"I'm sure he didn't know the difference. Deana was napping in the bedroom, and Jana was playing with her dilly-dolly in the floor. I tried to tell him that Jana wasn't his child, but he wouldn't believe me. He said I was lying. He snatched her up . . . and ran with her. Jason, I can't tell you how I felt!"

"Tell me everything you remember, Anna. Quickly."

"He wanted the land deed. He said that I had stolen the papers from him and that I had no rights to the Elliott land. He said that he was the legal owner through his child."

"Did you tell him—?"

"When I told him that I was the youngest daughter of the Elliott family, it made him very angry. He went into a rage, and his face was livid and twisted. He said that he was willing to *kill* for the land and that he would have it all: the property, the oil, and . . . and . . ." She covered her face again. "And *me.*"

Jason's hands formed fists. "And then he took our Jana?"

"He is holding her hostage until we turn the land deed over to him."

"Anna, a child—any child—is worth more than all the land and money in the world. We have been penniless before, and it will be no disgrace to live in poverty again. I have a strong back and two good hands, and I can make us a living almost anywhere. Lesley can have *everything* we own if we can just have Jana back. We must get that message across to him. Did he leave any means of contacting him?"

"None. But he will be back. He won't give up until . . . until we sign our rights away."

"I'm going into town and contact the law."

"Oh, no, Jason! No! He said if we told anyone, he would kill Jana and ask questions later. And he won't hesitate to carry out his threats. He has no conscience! Human life has no value to him. He has a . . . a deformed soul!"

"Then I will be sitting here when he comes back. The engine, the oil—none of that matters now."

It was a week before Lesley returned, but Jason had not left the house. "We must take care to never let Lesley see Deana, Anna," he said. "If he realizes he got the wrong child, he might try to kidnap her, too."

When Anna heard Lesley coming, she whisked Deana off to another room. "Shhh!" She put a finger to her lips. "Let's play *whisper.*"

195

"So now I get to talk to the big man of the house," Anna heard Lesley sneer. His slurred words tattled that he had been drinking. Anna stayed near the door so that she could hear.

"We want the child back," Jason began. "Where is she?"

"She's a long ways from here, and there's a price on her head."

"We are willing to pay it. Every penny."

"I'm glad to hear you say that, Jason Lewis, because the cost will be higher than you think. Besides this spread, I've decided that I want Anna Lewis thrown in on the deal. I should have had her in the first place, and there would be no dispute about the land now. You wooed her away from me."

"Watch your tongue, Lesley. You are tempting me."

A malevolent laugh leaped from Lesley's throat. "I'm not afraid of you, Jason. I have the child, remember. If you touch me, there will be no child to whimper."

"I could take this grand house and the money. But what good would a big house be without a *servant*? I want someone to wring out my clothes and iron them dry with a touch of starch. I want a cook that can make sourdough bread. And I want someone to warm up my back when it's cold at night. And I generally get what I want in the long run."

An open battle can be lost in a moment, but a silent battle always has a chance of being won, Jason thought. What kind of a diabolical scheme was this? "You can have anything you ask for *except my wife.*"

"Ah, Jason, you are a blockhead. I should have killed you back in Oklahoma and been rid of you. Like I told your wife, people who get in my way get cut down."

196

"You may take your leave now, Lesley. I don't allow that kind of talk in my home."

"I am to understand that you don't want the child?" he jeered.

"I've never seen greed with such filthy feet, Lesley. You can come back when you are sober, and we'll talk then."

"I'm sober—and we'll talk now."

Jason suddenly turned to a new tactic. "I'll tell you what, Lesley. If you want the responsibility of rearing a child that isn't even yours, so be it. Feed her and cloth her. Educate her. It will spare me the expense. But just remember one thing: if you harm her, you'll hang. I'll see to it. You made your threat and I heard it. *No one* pities a man who harms a child. *Anybody* will furnish a rope for his neck."

"You talk big, Jason. You know I don't want the kid. What I want is to be *right where you are*. And I plan to get there."

Even in the other room, Anna knew that Lesley's antagonism hit Jason head-on.

CHAPTER TWENTY-NINE

Willy

William wrote that he was coming on Tuesday, September 3. He wanted Jason to meet him at the stage stop in Mesilla. He said he could hardly wait to see Jana again.

"How will we tell him that Jana is . . . gone?" Just when Anna thought she'd conquered her tears, they came back with a new demand.

"I don't know how we'll break the dreadful news, Anna. The thought has been digging trenches in my mind ever since Lesley took her."

"Willy lost both of his parents and now . . . this. It will be too much. It will break his heart."

"I'm afraid so. I thought we would have heard from Lesley again by now and could work something out for her return."

"His silence gives me the creeps."

"It bodes no good, for sure. I pray for Jana's safety every day. This is when trust is . . . hard."

"Oh, Jason! Will the *night*, the *darkness*, never end? It seems *so long!*"

He took her in his arms. "It will end, my precious. I

don't know how or when. Only our Father knows that."

"You will go to pick up Willy?"

"Not alone. You and Deana will go with me. I wouldn't think of leaving you here for a single moment."

"But if we *both* leave, Jason, he might . . . he might set fire to the place . . . or something. Someone needs to stay and keep a busy eye on everything."

"The place is unimportant compared to you. Besides, I will need you to help me . . . comfort Willy. Telling him that Jana is not here will be like removing a precious object from a baby's fingers. His heart is bound up in the child like Jacob's heart was bound to little Benjamin in the Bible. I'm afraid William will be inconsolable."

Anna said little on the trip to town, but she snuggled close to Jason for solace. The trees preened their fall beauty, and she couldn't see past them. She considered them a parable of her present distress. She could see nothing but her troubles, with no vision beyond.

There seemed no way out of the black shadows of forest for her. Her world had been plunged into the darkness of night where there was no light and no time to hunt for one.

"I would like to drop Deana off at Mrs. Nagel's house, Jason," Anna said.

"You aren't afraid to leave her?"

"No. Lesley hasn't seen Deana and likely wouldn't recognize her if he did."

"Have you a reason for wanting to leave her?"

"Yes. With neither child along, Jana's absence won't be so blatant—such a sudden shock to Willy. We can discuss it without Deana hearing."

"You are a wise little mother, Anna."

"If Lesley did happen along, he would never know that Deana wasn't one of Mrs. Nagel's brood. Children do not interest him unless he has something to gain."

They left Deana to play with the younger Nagel children and went on to the coachhouse, arriving in time to welcome the incoming coach. The conveyance belched out three full-grown travelers.

"Where is Willy?" Anna asked.

One of the men, tall and muscular, bounded toward them in a long lope. It was William with his face-splitting grin.

"Willy Lewis! You've grown a foot!" Jason pumped his brother's broad and solid hand. "You are as tall as I am. How did this happen?"

William sobered. "I've had a long growing spell, brother. In more ways than one." His voice rode low in his throat. "But where is my pride and joy? I thought surely you'd bring her along to meet me!"

"We . . . we've lost her, William."

William's shoulders fell, and he seemed to wither inside. "You've *lost* her? I . . . I can't give her up, too! It's . . . it's too much! These last few weeks, I've lived just to see her again. When did she die and where did you bury her?"

"She isn't dead, but—"

"She's *alive*?"

"We believe that she is. Lesley Horn kidnapped her."

"Lesley Horn kidnapped my sister? Why would he want her? He has his own child, doesn't he?"

"Lesley thinks that he took his own child," Anna explained. "He didn't know that we had *two*. His child was sleeping in the back bedroom. He grabbed Jana and ran with her."

"But . . . *why*?"

"He is holding her for a ransom: our land. We're . . . we're trying to get her back, and we're willing to pay any price."

William's shoulders lifted to a defiant angle, and his eyes moved from Anna to Jason. "You told me once that Lesley Horn didn't have the stuff of a man in him, Jason. You told me that he talked out of both sides of his mouth and that he hadn't any ambition but to satisfy himself— that he had chicken feathers on him. I should never have listened to a word he said.

"He came looking for Anna, saying smooth-mouthed that he only wanted to see his child and would cause no trouble for anybody. It was I who told him where to find you. I am responsible for the kidnapping.

"Therefore, it will be my responsibility to find Lesley Horn and get Jana back." His face was etched with hard determination. "And God and I will do it!"

"I have not been able to go looking for Lesley because I couldn't abandon Anna and Deana—" Jason began.

"But I can search relentlessly," William said. "I've tracked animals and birds and trapped them. Lesley cannot hide forever. Do you think he is still in this part of the country?"

"We haven't heard from him in several days, but I'm sure he's still around. He said, though, that he had taken Jana a long ways off."

"If she is anywhere in the world, I will find her."

As they passed down Main Street, Mr. Fleming flagged them to a stop. "Are you aware that there's a man in town trying to break the will Mr. Elliott left for Anna?"

"We have heard that someone would like to have the

land," replied Jason with caution.

"This man claims to have rights through his deceased wife by virtue of a child. He wants ready cash and has hired a snaky lawyer to get it for him."

"We will be fair in the matter when it comes to the child's part, Mr. Fleming," Jason said. "But we will not tolerate anyone pushing past the point of fairness."

"Perhaps you should hire an attorney to protect your interests."

Anna's mind somersaulted back to Lesley's warning. "Thank you, Mr. Fleming. We will handle it. We will . . . make it a matter of prayer."

They returned to Mrs. Nagel's for Deana. "Have you ever had a man boarder with scraped-back hair and piercing eyes?" Anna asked her.

"Yes'm. Some weeks past a'ready. A Mr. Horn. An' he most nigh had horns a'ready yet. He set my teeth edgin'. He all stayed a night, though. But when he came with an addict to corn squeezins under his tongue a'ready, I turned him off. Refused him another night's let under my roof a'ready. It wonders me where he is roostin' now." She shook her head. "I shoulda sicked th' law on him. Is someone takin' their head in to find him a'ready?"

"He kidnapped our Jana!"

"Lawsy, no! Should I see him, Miz Lewis, I'll spike him to a first post a'ready!"

"Thank you, Mrs. Nagel. Please do that. My husband's younger brother, William, has come to live with us. He is quite upset over Jana, and he will be helping us search for her."

"Is th' boy job-needin'?"

"He'll likely work for Jason."

"Jake yenned to th' city a'ready an' that lets me all anymore fer a driver fer th' milk route. Till December a'ready, Jake will be nineteen an' he yens to sit Sundays with a girlie a'ready. Ain't nobody here that hearts his fancy onct your Jason let back here an' tuk you back a'ready. Jake was glad, yet sored, about that. But since he left a'ready, I'm bad fer some help."

"Willy might be able to help you for a few days."

"I'd pay by percent a'ready—an' him figure."

"I'll tell him."

William was buoyant enough until he reached the house. Then his glittering hope faded before the somber reality. When he saw Jana's dilly-dolly that he had made laying on the table, he turned briskly and walked outside along a trail of crushed grass.

CHAPTER THIRTY

The Finding of an Evil Man

Jason found the scrawled note near the front stoop. Horror lurked in the printed words; they were as rancid as the paper on which they were written.

"You are never far from me, Anna," the message said. "But soon you will be even closer. Soon now I will decide it is time that your husband must be put out of the way. It will not please you at first, but you will be glad later. When he is gone, I will go for the child and bring her back to you—after we have had some time alone." The note was signed "L.H."

"Jason, I'm . . . I'm scared right into my spinal column." Images churned in Anna's mind.

"What time I am afraid, I will trust in thee. Remember, Anna?"

"I'll try. Where is Willy?"

"He has to have some time to himself to sort out his feelings. That was always Willy's way. You will recall that even as a youngster, he would roam out and hunt horned toads when he was bothered in his spirit. He'll be back."

The sun was a blurred yellow disk, its rays westering,

when William came in. His eyes were red and swollen. "I think I found Maw and Paw's cabin," he told Jason, "between here and the river."

"Yes, that's it."

"They would have been happy there. Has someone lived there recently?"

"No one has lived there since Maw and Paw. Anna fixed it up for a playhouse—"

"There are bottles littered all around, and I know Paw never drank a drop. And I'm sure Anna wouldn't leave such a mess. There's a tablet and a quill, too, with the ink not dried. It smelled terrible in there, like something rotten."

"Jason—" Anna reeled, and Jason balanced her with a supportive hug. "It's . . . him."

"Were there any signs of . . . a child, Willy?"

"No, nothing except for a quilt."

"That's Deana's quilt," Anna whispered.

"If you'll stay with Anna, William, I will go up to the cabin first thing in the morning and see—"

"No, Jason, please don't go! Lesley will harm you! Let me go instead!"

Anna's judgment was dimmed by the pallor of stark fright. Jason soothed her hair. "I'm not afraid of Lesley Horn, Anna. He is a coward, and I have a God who will protect me. And God made a man to protect a woman— and that's what I plan to do."

"Yes, but Jason, once in Oklahoma he was going to shoot you in the *back*. He can't be trusted!"

"No, he can't. But God can. I'm still alive, am I not?'

"Jason—"

"The reason I haven't already turned Lesley Horn to sausage is because he has our Jana. I don't want to nettle him and reduce our chances of getting her back. I've been walking a tight wire, playing along with his foolishness. But he has pushed his luck too far. I won't have him bringing his grog onto our property!"

Jason was awake most of the night trying to allay Anna's worst fears. Only when he prayed for her did the demons retreat. He overslept the next morning, and when he awoke, William was out and gone. There was a whisper of dampness in the air, and the early morning sun was caught in a web of clouds.

A note had been pushed under the front door. "Beautiful Anna," Lesley's note read, "Today is the day that your husband will get to shake hands with Saint Peter. That will make three people happy: Saint Peter, your husband, and me. Soon all will be mine and yours. Do not cry. The child is safe."

Jason stuffed the vile note in his pocket. *Anna must not see it!*

Poor Anna. Her frayed nerves could stand little more. If only he could spare her this suffering. . . .

A scoundrel like Lesley wasn't worthy to be called a man. If one wanted that title, he must be *honest* and *trustworthy*. A true man didn't prey on women and small children, frightening and threatening them. A real man would be honorable, choosing death over dishonor. There wasn't an ounce of manhood in Lesley's crab-apple soul.

Jason didn't find Lesley at the cottage. He found a half-empty bottle and more notes scattered about the floor. A loaded gun in its holster and a tobacco pouch filled with bullets lay on the makeshift bed. Jason confiscated the weapon and its ammunition. Anna would be relieved to know that Lesley was unarmed. Jason was relieved, too. Who knew when the deranged man might try to shoot Anna?

The notes about the floor were in various stages of completion. They were crude notes meant for Anna but not fit for a lady's eyes. Some were obviously a product of a drunken stupor; they made no sense at all. The lot of them made Jason furious. He tore them to shreds. He wished he could find Lesley and give him a proper thrashing. Now that he was away from Anna, he'd make Lesley Horn dance and talk. He'd tell where Jana was . . . or wish he had!

Jason waited an hour for Lesley's return, his righteous indignation mounting by degrees. He waited another hour, sure that Lesley would return to finish off the waiting bottle. But when Lesley didn't show up, he decided he dare not wait longer. Anna would be awake and worrying herself ill if he did not show up at home within a reasonable time.

A week passed, and no more notes appeared. Each day, either Jason or William checked on the cabin. The telltale bottle kept its contents, unimbibed. As the days passed like snails, Anna ate little, slept less. The shadows under her eyes grew darker. Her "night" had been so long, she told Jason, that she felt bankrupt and empty with no resources left to draw from.

It was William who discovered Lesley's body. "I found him, Jason."

"Where?"

"At the river. Washed up on the brown edge of its skirt. He's dead."

"Drowned," supplied Jason. "He was probably trying to catch some fish. Or mayhap he tried to have a swim while he was drunk."

Anna's tears fell quietly like her nature. "I am thankful that there will be no more notes and no more threats, Jason," she said, "but now we'll never know where our Jana is. He took the knowledge with him to eternity."

"I'll find her, Anna." William's voice was gruff with emotion, "if it takes me the rest of my life!"

"We'll have to dispose of the body, William," Jason said.

"Bury him here on the land, Jason," Anna suggested.

"No. That wouldn't be fair to you, Anna. While he was alive, he brought you too much heartache."

"Vengeance and hatred are barren things," Anna said. "After all, he was Deana's natural father—and I want her to remember him not as he was, but as he could have been had he not been marked by the branding iron of sin."

"Anna, my darling. You amaze me. I've never seen such a heart of charity and forgiveness. We will honor your wishes."

"And we'll have a little ceremony, Jason. Deana is old enough to remember."

"Come, William, we'll dig the grave down by the cabin." Jason turned to go for the shovel and William followed.

CHAPTER THIRTY-ONE

The Milk Route

Leonainie Nagel fascinated William. He considered her a paragon of beauty. The fact that she was shy and "never got her tongue when there were guests" only gave her the greater mystique, made her seem the more celestial to him. It galled him that she was expected to drive the milk wagon in her truant brother's place.

It wasn't the job for a lady. It was too dangerous and too strenuous. He thought less of Jake Nagel for abandoning his mother and the younger children for his own ambitions. William's own manly qualities wouldn't abide watching Leonainie struggle through fear and dread to do a man's job.

"I'll take the route for a few days until you can advertise in the county paper for a proper driver," he told Mrs. Nagel. "Leonainie is more suited for softer work."

"You are a God-sent a'ready, Will-*yum*," she said.

Mrs. Nagel's ethereal baby, whose skin looked transparent, attached herself to William. She called him "Weeyum." Her large, liquid eyes reminded William of a kitten he had seen in Lubbock.

"She's tuk in her head fer someone to 'friend 'er since

her paw's all any more to heaven," Mrs. Nagel told him. "And you're all in fer it."

"I'll be glad to be her friend, Mrs. Nagel," he promised. "I've always liked *little people*. The next time Jason and I go to Las Cruces, I'll try to get some empty spools from the millinery and make her a dilly-dolly. I made my little sister one, and I made Anna's little girl one."

"*Little people!*" Mrs. Nagel threw back her head and gave a rippling laugh. "You got a funny tongue in yur head a'ready! Sissy's pined fer a dolly, but I couldn't let the money for one a'ready."

"She'll have a dolly made by Willy."

Meanwhile, William left no stone unturned in his search for Jana. He contacted the stage manager and asked if there had been a man and child leave Mesilla in the past few weeks. The man said there hadn't been, and he had such a memory for passengers that he would have remembered them. He remembered back two and half years when Jason came in with Jana. "A lone man with a child is a spectacle one doesn't soon forget," the man said. "One suspects there has been a tragedy of a lost wife and mother, and one's sympathy is spurred and goes to bucking."

When William described Lesley, the manager said, yes, there had been a man come in that fit the description, but he hadn't staged out.

Next William went to the new lawyer in town. "Was a Mr. Horn a client of yours?" he asked, using no sidesteps.

"I don't discuss my clients with strangers, young man."

"Mr. Horn isn't your client."

"And what do you know of Mr. Horn *or* my clients?"

The lawyer's yellow-green eyes, lost between slits in the bulbous pouches of his face, seemed as opaque as marbles.

"I know plenty. More than you do. If he's anybody's client, he's the devil's."

The lawyer tried to turn the tables on William, but William could be cagey, too.

"Oh, come now—"

"Lesley Horn is in eternity now."

"He was only in to see me a few days ago and we discussed . . . well, never mind what we discussed."

"I know what you discussed. A few days ago he was alive. Today he is dead. It doesn't take but a few seconds to die."

"He *can't* be dead. He promised me a thousand dollars if I would come to Mesilla and represent him in the case of—he had a legitimate case with the law on his side! I borrowed the money to set up this office to handle his affairs!" The attorney's face became suffused, the veins on his temple swelled.

"Mayhap you should close your doors and start paying that loan back."

"Look. I'd have to have some proof and not just some upstart's word—"

"I have plenty of proof. I can call my brother in. We dug Mr. Horn's grave and attended his funeral."

"I wonder how he thinks I'll get that money he promised with him up and dead?"

"That could be a problem. Where is Lesley Horn's child?"

"This is a frame-up. He told me to beware—"

"If you'd like, we can call the sheriff. Mr. Horn kidnapped a child, and it was the wrong one."

The opaque eyes shifted. "I never saw a child. He told me that he had one—we were building a lawsuit around her—but I don't know where she lived. He never did say. And that's the honest truth even if it did come out of my mouth."

"Thank you, sir." William started out the door.

"Wait a minute, young man. When and where and how did he die—?"

William heard him but chose to ignore his inquiries. He didn't like the pettifogger. It was obvious that he knew nothing about Jana. He hurried on his way to deliver more milk.

William's route covered seventeen homes in Mesilla and on its outskirts. Many of the families had small children, and they swarmed about William when he made his deliveries.

The Carver family had a crippled child, an undersized boy of about eight. William was touched with pity for the boy, and he tried to think what he could do to make the child happy, to make his days abed less tedious. What would it be like to lie on a couch day in and day out while the other children romped and played?

Most boys didn't care for dolls. But if he could make a doll of spools, why not a horse? The thought pulled his mouth into a smile as he mentally assembled legs and a tail and a head.

"Adam, would you like a toy horse to play with?" he asked the boy.

The child's small gaunt face lighted with an inner spark. "Will ya make me a horsey, Willy? Will ya, Willy? I'd be so glad, I'd play with it all day and all night and even on Sunday if Mama would let me," he said.

214

"When I get some spools, I'll make you one."

Every Saturday was spent in town. William walked the streets, watching each child that came and went. He'd back himself against a post and ready his eyes for each pedestrian with a lassie. But none of them was Jana. *My heart will tell me when I find her*, he told himself.

Oh God, he prayed, *please help me.*

Chapter Thirty-Two

So Long the Night

"I haven't seen any little girls that look like I think Jana would look now," he told Anna when his search took him through the turning of another calendar's leaf, putting them into October. "Do you think I would even recognize her if I saw her? It has been so long—"

"I believe you'll know her when you see her, William," Anna assured. "She's still small for her age, and she looks much the same as she did when she was younger. She has the same head of black curls, only they've grown longer. She has a dimple when she smiles, but just one. It's on the left side. She has a tiny scar that one would hardly notice on the side of her hand where she touched the stove last year."

"You don't suppose that Lesley took her back to Oklahoma, do you?"

"He wasn't gone long enough between visits, notes and threats to make such a lengthy trip. Anyhow, I wrote to Philip Horn about his son's death and asked him to notify us if he had Jana. I told him that Lesley had picked her up by mistake thinking she was his own child and that I still have Lesley's child. I let him know that we were very eager to get Jana back. Mr. Horn is a good man. He would have contacted us before now if he had the wrong grand-daughter."

"As soon as Mrs. Nagel can find a replacement for me on the milk route, I'll spread out and look for her in some other areas. Today I'm making up some wanted posters. They'll say: 'Lost. Three-year-old girl with black curls and dark eyes who answers to the name of Jana.'" He stopped. "Can we give a reward?"

"Name any amount of money you wish, William."

"That might bring a worm out of the woodwork."

"It might."

"Do you know when Jason is going to Las Cruces again?"

"We'll ask him."

"I want to go, too. Besides taking the posters, I want to pick up some empty spools. I have something special in mind. I want to make all the children on the milk route a toy for Christmas. I can make dolls and horses and birds and trains. I like making little people happy!"

William lapsed into silence. The thought of making his "little people" happy tossed his mind to a small boy named Bubba at the end of his route. The child had big, sad eyes; he had never seen the youngster smile. An older sister, already in the first primer, chattered like a magpie, but the boy had never spoken a word. *Mayhap he is deaf,* William thought.

If only he could make that one child happy! What could he make that would draw out the wee fellow so turned within himself? Sadness was worse than crippled limbs. He bared his problem to Anna.

Anna suggested a train with a smiling face. She would

paint the face if William would construct the engine, she said. Even if the little boy couldn't hear, he could see the locomotive's cheery message. A toy might teach him to smile.

That week, a young man who moved to Mesilla from San Miguel answered Mrs. Nagel's ad for a driver. He looked sturdy and dependable, but William cringed when he grinned at Leonainie in a too-friendly manner. William felt more comfortable, though, when Leonainie turned her face toward *him* and gave him a sweet, tender smile. That smile prompted William to promise Mrs. Nagel that he would drop by and see her "little people" every Saturday when he came to town.

Anna had a letter from Mary Butler, and she shared the news with Jason and William at the supper table. Mary wept with joy that Jason was alive. She had her children and claimed that her "joy was unspeakable and full of stories." Then she shared yards and yards of the stories with Anna. The stories made them all laugh.

"Mary's letters are a star in my black night," Anna told Jason. "But I am so eager to see the light of day again!"

Jason brought in another small oil well, and life dropped back into its usual order. But the pain of Jana's absence did not lessen with time. Indeed, it seemed to increase. They all dreaded facing the holidays with her missing. The night wore on, long and dark.

By the middle of November, William had taken his posters to Las Cruces, San Miguel, Leasburg, Los Corralitos, Radium Springs, and as far north as Hatch. He watched the mail every day for a response, but there was none.

William went to work on his Christmas toys. He and Jason found a place in El Paso that manufactured spools, and Jason bought William a whole crate of them. Tables, cabinets and shelves were lined with them, but Anna didn't mind. The project was therapy for William.

William saved the making of Bubba's train until last. It was his "special creation," and he prayed that it would make the sorrowful child smile.

When delivery time came, he chose Caballocita and the shay for the trip, hoping to coax Leonainie to accompany him on his care mission. Bubba's "happy train" would be his last gift stop. *And then mayhap Mrs. Nagel will invite me in for wassail,* his mind supplied.

Leonainie rode beside him, prim and ladylike, and leaned his way on the corners. He wished there were more corners.

The toys brought squeals and hand clapping from the little people and words of appreciation from the grateful mothers. "It was such a lovely thing to do," Leonainie said.

"We're coming to the most special one, Leonainie," he said, liking the taste of her name when he said it. "The little boy who lives here never talks or smiles. He has a . . . a *lost* look in his eyes. His name is Bubba, and I'm not sure that he can hear or speak. I made him a train, and Anna painted a face on it. It turned out wonderfully! Oh, I do hope that he likes it!"

"He will," she said. "A body would like anything *you* made!"

The words warmed William's insides. He made a mental note to go home and carve out a hairpin box for her. Shaped like a heart?

"Please go with me to the house," he invited when he reached the last residence. He took her hand and helped her from the buggy, thrilling at her dependence on the strength of his arm.

Bubba came to the door, hiding behind his older sister, who hid behind her mother.

"I have something for your children," William said. "Christmas gifts."

"Come on in, William," she urged. "And bring your lady friend."

"This is Leonainie Nagel," he said and stepped back and held the door for her. Out of his sack he pulled the dilly-dolly he had made for the older girl, but exactly what happened next he was never quite able to remember in sequence.

The sad-eyed boy screamed, "My dilly-dolly! My Willy made it!"

William stared at the boy. Could it be—? The child ran to William with a radiant smile. And when he smiled, there was the dimple on the left side of his face. He took "Bubba's" right hand and searched for the scar. It was where Anna said it would be.

"Jana!" he cried, and she jerked her head up in instant response to her name. Now he recognized her eyes. And her face was the same even without the curly locks of hair.

She ran into his outstretched arms. "Are you my Willy?" she asked.

"I'm your Willy!" He held her as if he could never let her go.

The woman looked bewildered. "That's the first words the child has spoken. Do you know . . . her?"

"She's my sister! I'm her Willy, and I will take her home with me."

"Oh, but you can't! The man said . . ."

"Whatever anybody says, she belongs to me."

221

"He said that I must not let *anyone* have her—"

"This is not Mr. Horn's child. He *thought* she was his when he took her, but he picked up the wrong lassie. I have wanted posters out for Jana in several counties."

The woman blanched. "I didn't know. . . . The man said he would pay me a thousand dollars if I would keep her and not tell that she wasn't a boy. He . . . he had her hair cut and had her garbed in a boy's knickers when he brought her to me. Once when he came he was gripping a bottle as if it could hold him upright. I scolded him for that. No child should have a bottle-hooked paw. He allowed as how he was so lonely for his dead wife and that was the first time he'd ever got drunk and he promised he'd never do it again. Then I felt shamed for making him feel badly in his grief."

"To Mr. Horn, lying was simply an exercise of a right. He could make anyone who didn't know him believe that elephants have wings."

"He used to come to check up on this child every week, but it's been a long while since he's been here. I've been worried—"

"The reason he hasn't been here is because he is dead. He drowned in the Rio Grande River out on my brother's place."

"Then I'll *never* get my money?"

"I'll see that you get a fair wage for keeping my sister, ma'am, but a thousand dollars is a bit overpriced for baby-sitting."

"Oh, I wouldn't expect much. Just enough for her food and keep."

"You'll have your pay within the week."

Leonainie stood holding the smiling engine, absorbed

in William's mounting joy. He had forgotten about the toy.

"Let us be on our way, Leonainie. God has just given me the best Christmas gift a fellow could ever ask for!"

Jana sang to her dilly-dolly all the way to Leonainie's house. "I can't stay this time," William told Leonainie. "But if your maw will let me, I'll come and sit Sunday after church."

Pure devotion outshone Leonainie's shyness. "Mama's new driver asked me, and I wouldn't sit with *him*."

William's shirt tightened about his chest. That girl had a way of making a fellow feel like the governor.

Jana was asleep, still clutching her doll when they got to the ranch. William began yelling as he went through the door. "Anna! Jason! The curls didn't come with her, but here she is!"

Jana roused and saw Anna. "Mommy . . ." she murmured. "My dilly-dolly . . . Willy made it . . ." Her eyes closed in blissful sleep again.

"Jason!" Anna rushed to his side. "The long night is over!"

"Yes, my love." He held her in his arms. "Here in the west they say 'So long' when they bid someone goodbye. We'll say, *So long, the night!*"